A SAFE PLACE TO SLEEP

a novel by

JENNIFER L. JORDAN

Our Power Press

First edition.
10-9-8-7-6-5-4-3-2-1

This is a work of fiction. Any similarity to persons living or dead is a coincidence.

Published by:
Our Power Press
P.O. Box 6680
Denver, Colorado 80206

ISBN 0-9634075-0-3

*For all the children
who grew up
in the night*

I've waited a long time to tell this story. If it were just her story, I could have told it years ago.

Her name was Destiny Greaves. She was a strong, beautiful woman who hired me to look into her past.

I wasn't prepared for what I found in her past... or in mine. But then, how could anyone have prepared for what we discovered? Such loss. Such gain. In such a short span of time. I've often wondered if there are limits to the amount of pain and joy human beings can feel. I think I found my own limit on this case.

I wonder if Destiny found hers.

Sometimes, I like to think back to that very first day, to the day when I first heard about her. It was a day full of such hope.

I remember it as if it were yesterday....

CHAPTER

1

It was an unusually warm Sunday afternoon in late February. I'd just returned from an exhausting thirty-mile bike ride through the streets of Denver. The phone was ringing as I opened my apartment door. I propped my mountain bike against the living room wall and ran to catch the call before my answering machine did. I just made it.

"Kris, you're never going to believe this — I met the most incredible woman at the Book Garden yesterday!" my friend Michelle gushed.

"Hold on a sec, Michelle, I just got in."

I set the phone down, took the keys out of the door and wheeled my mountain bike out onto the nineteenth floor balcony. I tossed my bike helmet on the couch, walked into the kitchen, and poured myself a stiff drink — Dr. Pepper on shaved ice — as a reward for having exercised intensely. All of this, I did at a leisurely pace. Over the years, I'd heard enough of Michelle's descriptions of women she'd met. Invariably, they were long and excruciatingly detailed. No sense hurrying for one.

I plopped down on the couch and massaged my rubbery legs which were still cool from the crisp Colorado air.

"Okay."

"Geez, Kris, did you clean your whole apartment?"

I ignored her question. She'd seen my apartment. She knew I couldn't clean it in a full day of hard labor much less in three scant minutes.

"Tell me about this woman."

That simple request magically restored her good humor.

"I'm in love, Kris. I swear it. This time, I'm in love."

"I'm sure you are." Michelle fell in love more often than most people grocery shop.

"I know what you're thinking," she said, as if reading my mind across the phone lines. "It's another one of Michelle's silly crushes, but this time, it's different. At least it feels different."

"What's her name?" I asked as I restyled my "helmet" hair, using a nearby spoon as a mirror.

"Destiny Greaves."

"Yeah, right. Real funny!"

"I'm serious."

"Oh, sure," I answered, completely unable to believe that my friend Michelle had met the most famous lesbian in Denver.

"Kris, c'mon, I'm not kidding you."

"Are you talking about *the* Destiny Greaves, the one who's an activist, the one we see on TV all the time?"

"Exactly."

"The one who runs the Lesbian Community Center?"

"Yes, yes, that's who I met."

"The one who's tall, blonde, and incredibly beautiful?"

"Even more so in person than on TV."

"Wow!" Now that she had me convinced, I was impressed. "By the way, what were you doing at the Book Garden? You don't even like to read." I loudly slurped my drink.

"Women's bookstores are not just about reading," Michelle said as if she were explaining the most simple idea to a child. "I went to an author's lecture yesterday to meet women."

"What author?"

"Who knows? She was quite boring. I can't even remember her name. Anyway, after the reading, several women stayed around to browse and chat. That's when I met Destiny. I went right up and told her I thought she was an interesting person, and I'd like to get to know her better."

"What did she say?"

"Well, first she laughed. But then, she asked me what my name was. I'd been thinking so hard about what I was going to say that I forgot to tell her my name. Anyway, we couldn't talk in the Book Garden because everyone was standing around, and a lot of women were staring at her. All the attention seemed to make her uncomfortable, so the next thing I knew, she asked me out to lunch. I'd already eaten, but I gladly accepted. We had a great lunch — she's a fantastic woman. She's done so much with her life."

"Hmm." I tried to think of more to say, but I was too shocked. Michelle Spivack and Destiny Greaves. How odd!

"And you'll never believe this, Kris. The best part of all is that she's not in a relationship!"

"That is good," I said. For Michelle, it was not only good, it was a veritable miracle. She had a bad habit of falling in love with women who were already in relationships or otherwise unavailable.

"I can't wait for you to meet her."

"Isn't this jumping the gun a little, Michelle? I mean you only met her yesterday. Did you even set up another date?"

"Of course we did. We're going to dinner tomorrow night."

"Did she ask you out or did you ask her?"

"I asked her," she said, sounding a bit disappointed. "But she seemed glad I asked and she said 'yes' right away."

"That's a good sign."

"She's so much like you. It freaked me out talking to her — you're even the same age. You are twenty-nine now, aren't you?"

"Yes," I said tersely. Michelle could never remember my age, or my birthday for that matter, though she never forgot my astrological sign.

"Also, she's a Libra."

"Great!" I said with more than a trace of sarcasm.

"I know you don't believe in that stuff, but there's a lot of truth in it. I can see the similarities in you and Destiny!"

"Like what?"

"She sees things in a completely different way, just like you do. She spots opportunities where none exist and then somehow, she pulls them off. After lunch, we went to my house, and I read her Tarot cards, and they came up like yours always come up."

"With lots of money cards showing?"

"Exactly."

"Are you sure you were reading them correctly?" I didn't mean to offend, but Michelle had only recently learned to read Tarot cards, and she was often unsure of what the cards meant. I let her practice on me and tried not to take her too seriously.

"I think so. But that's not the most exciting part. Guess what happened after I read her cards. Just try to guess!"

"I give up," I said without trying.

5

"C'mon, Kris, guess!"

"All right, all right... you made mad, passionate love."

"How did you know?" she sounded disappointed.

"Because you always do."

"This time, it was different. I didn't even put the moves on her. We were sitting on my couch, and she leaned toward me and told me she wanted to make love with me, but she didn't want to marry me."

"What the hell's that supposed to mean? Of course she didn't want to marry you. She just met you."

"What she meant was that some women view love-making as a commitment. She doesn't. She wanted to enjoy making love with me without feeling bad when she couldn't make an emotional commitment. That's exactly what she said."

"Huh. What did you say to that?"

"I didn't know what to say. No one has ever been that honest with me. I did ask her if she'd just ended a long-term relationship, but she said she'd never been in one."

"Why not?"

"I didn't ask. Should I have?"

"Of course, you should have!" I practically shouted. "Don't you want to be in a long-term relationship? Aren't you trying to break your cycle of becoming involved with women who are never available, like Amber and Joyce and Karen...?" I could have gone on with the list, but I didn't have the heart.

"Do you think it's a bad sign?"

"Yes, Michelle," I replied with exaggerated patience.

"Maybe she's been busy with her work."

"I'm sure she has."

"Maybe I can change that in her."

"I'm sure you can't."

"Really?" she asked, even though she knew the answer.

"Really!" I said emphatically. And I'd had such high hopes for Michelle with this one.

"Well anyway, Kris, I still can't believe it. Me and Destiny Greaves. My psychic told me I'd be meeting someone important, but I never dreamed I'd be dating her."

Frankly, I couldn't believe it either. When the week before Michelle had told me about her appointment with the psychic, what she said went right in one ear and out the other. Because I didn't believe in this woman's ability to predict the future (she was right so seldom, I think I could have done a better job of it

6

myself), I rarely listened to what she said. Michelle, on the other hand, always thought her word was gospel.

For once, the psychic, who was also her hairdresser (another reason I distrusted her), seemed to be right. And in a big way.

From a distance, I'd followed Destiny Greaves' accomplishments. If she wasn't in the daily papers for her scathing assessment of the governor's insensitivity to the AIDS crisis, she was on the nightly news fighting for equal access for disabled people, or in the gay press chastising NOW for its discrimination against lesbians. She seemed to be fighting every important battle that was going on in Denver and winning most of them.

Years ago, I'd heard there were death threats against her, but if that was true, they didn't slow her down a bit. She was as vocal and vociferous as ever.

I could see what Michelle saw in Destiny, but I wondered privately what Destiny saw in Michelle. I hoped, for my friend's sake, that her feelings would be requited.

Several weeks passed before I actually met Destiny, and when I did it was under strange circumstances. Michelle kept setting up dinners for the three of us and cancelling them. Finally, she told me why. Destiny wanted to meet me alone. And ours would not be a social meeting.

Destiny Greaves wanted to hire me.

CHAPTER

2

Destiny didn't want to hire me to do the kind of work that occupied most of my days — designing marketing materials for health care practitioners. No indeed! Her request was much more unusual... and much more interesting!

Michelle arranged our first meeting but didn't attend. It took place at my office, a small comfortable storefront near Washington Park.

"So you're Destiny Greaves," I greeted her, when she walked through the front door, exactly on time. I offered her my hand and my best smile.

"And you're Kristin Ashe," she countered, as she shook my hand warmly and returned my smile.

I ushered Destiny into my private office, which really wasn't very private. Glass windows on one side looked out into a reception area; on the other, a graphics department. All the windows had mini-blinds, but I seldom lowered them. Secretly, I would have felt more comfortable with them closed, but I was forever trying to imitate the open, relaxed style of management that I read about in entrepreneurial magazines.

After combining all the piles on my couch into one, I offered Destiny a seat. I noted with interest that she sat on the side of the couch closest to me.

"Michelle's told me a lot about you."

"Likewise," I said, leaning back in my chair. "In fact," I added with perhaps a trace of jealousy, "she talks about you all the time— when she's not seeing you, that is."

"I hope it's good."

"Are you kidding, it's great," I said truthfully. "So how is Michelle? I haven't seen her since...God, how long has it been... since the night before last."

Destiny laughed politely.

"She's fine. She said to tell you 'hello'."

"Oh sure, like she can't wait two more hours to tell me herself. If I know Michelle, she'll call me five minutes after you've left here and ask me what I think of you."

For a second, I thought Destiny herself would ask me what I thought, but she didn't. Instead, she gave me a bemused look.

"I've heard a lot of good things about you, too, Kris."

"Michelle talks too much."

"Not just from Michelle. I read the article about you in *The Colorado Business Journal*. 'Young Entrepreneur of the Year.' Not bad!"

"I paid them to write it," I joked, but secretly, I was glad Destiny had seen the article. I was proud of what I'd accomplished. At the age of twenty-one, I'd started my own company with five hundred dollars, some good ideas, and a tremendous amount of ignorance and energy. Eight years later, I was the president of a company that did half a million a year in sales, employed five other women, and afforded me the opportunity to pursue other interests.

"Michelle thinks we have a lot in common," she said, leaning forward, almost challenging me.

"Because we're twenty-nine and we're both Libras." I nodded.

"Do you believe in astrology?"

"Not much. Do you?"

"Not really. I believe mostly in things I can see. I'm very practical that way. But Michelle's trying to teach me."

"Are you learning anything?"

"Only that I'm more skeptical and close-minded than I knew." We both laughed.

"I have to admit," Destiny said coyly, "Michelle did tell me about your famous Christmas ping-pong tournaments."

"Did she tell you she's never won?"

"She did. She also told me you're the most competitive person she ever met."

Probably because she's lost so many times, I thought but didn't say.

The past four years, Michelle and I had played a ten-game tournament on Christmas day. Each year, we bet one hundred dollars. All Michelle had to do to win the bet was win one game, yet she never did it. My streak was unbroken at forty games. And counting. The irony was that we were fairly closely matched in terms of skill. Michelle kept right up with me, point for point, but she could never win, maybe because winning wasn't important enough to her, and it was everything to me.

"She probably exaggerated," I said, forever trying to excuse my competitiveness.

"I like women who are competitive. They're so rare."

"No kidding?" I perked up. "Did Michelle also tell you that when I was in fifth grade, I sold more Girl Scout cookies than my whole troop combined?"

"She did." She laughed easily. "But how did you know?"

"She tells everyone that story. It's her favorite story about me. She likes it that at the age of nine, I thought to open up a new market. While all the other scouts were selling to their parents and neighbors, I was selling to office workers."

"You were a woman ahead of your time."

"I was. Unfortunately, it was all for naught. The executive director that year embezzled all the money."

"Oh, no!"

"Oh, yes. It was quite the scandal. The Girl Scouts gave me my first lessons, good and bad, in business."

"I was in Brownies for a year, then they kicked me out. I think I was too much of a rebel then."

"You still are."

"I am, aren't I?" She laughed.

As she laughed, I took a moment to look at her more closely. Her blonde hair was long, straight and neatly brushed back into a simple ponytail. Her dress was casual that day: tailored pants, cotton shirt, wool blazer, and penny loafers. Maybe it was my imagination, but once when I looked at her, she looked like a young Lauren Bacall.

Michelle had told me Destiny had a "hot body," so I'd been expecting a beautiful woman. But my friend had neglected to tell me how much character resided in her face. There was depth in her green eyes. Her forehead, in particular, fascinated me. In its tall majesty registered signs of laughter, concern, confusion, and more. Every range of emotion could easily be read across the plane of her head as it wrinkled with expression.

11

"I suppose Michelle told you why I'm here."

"She said you wanted to hire me, but she didn't tell me why."

"I asked her not to."

"She didn't."

"Good." Destiny sounded relieved. "To tell you the truth, I'm a little embarrassed to be here. I debated whether or not to come. I wasn't sure I would until I walked through that door." She inclined her head toward the front door.

"I know what I do seems a little weird," I offered, trying to put her at ease. "Michelle did tell you what I do, didn't she?"

"She told me in your spare time you do detective work for women. Is that right?" She uncrossed the legs that she'd just crossed.

"Sort of. I helped a woman locate an ex-lover. I helped another one get her job back. I even did one lesbian divorce case — one was enough!"

"Why do you do it? You obviously have a successful business here with this company."

"You know, no one's ever asked me that. I guess I do it to keep from being bored... and to help people. To pay the bills I own this company, Marketing Consultants. At one time, this was my income and my passion, now it's mostly my income. I have a high need to be constantly challenged. Once I learned how to run a business, the challenge was gone."

"How did you get started doing this other thing, what you do for women?"

"By accident really. My friend Terri asked me to help her find a woman she'd met through the personals. With a little skill and a lot of luck, I was successful. One thing led to another, and here I am."

"Do you like doing this?" She looked at me doubtfully.

"I love it."

"Hmm," she said, still sounding skeptical.

"I've helped a lot of women," I said quietly but firmly. "I can probably help you."

"But my request is so strange," she said as if she were wishing she'd never met me.

"Lay it on my brain and I'll tell you if I can help. If I can, I will. If not, we'll go out to lunch and talk about Michelle."

Through her nervousness, she smiled.

"Okay. I want you to help me find my parents."

"They're lost! You misplaced your parents? Shame on you!"

"No," she protested, the humor easing her tension. She took a deep breath. "I'm adopted. I want you to help me find out more about my natural parents."

"You want me to help you track them down? Find out who they are? Don't they have agencies that will help you search?"

"No, no, nothing like that. I know who they are...."

I raised my eyebrows.

"They're Barbara and Peter Kenwood."

"Do you know where they are?"

"Of course," she said in a detached tone.

"Where? Are they still together?"

"They're side by side." She paused for effect. "On the east end of Fairmount Cemetery."

If her intention had been to shock me, it worked. I put down the paper clip I'd been fiddling with and sat up in my chair.

"How long have they been there?"

"Almost twenty-five years."

"How did they die?"

"In a car crash, I've been told. They were driving home from a Christmas party in Conifer. Another car crossed over the line and hit them head on. They both died instantly. That's all I know. I was four at the time, but I don't remember anything about the accident. That's why I want to hire you. I want you to help me find out what my parents were like. I want to know more about them, what kind of people they were, who their friends were. I want to get to know these people who raised me the first four years of my life."

"Were there any other relatives? Of the Kenwoods, I mean?"

"I don't know."

"You were their only child?"

"As far as I know."

"You don't remember?"

She shook her head.

"Can you remember anything?"

"No, I have a complete and total memory loss. I can't remember a single thing about my life before the age of four."

A chill went up my spine. I picked up the paper clip again and began furiously bending and unbending it.

"Nothing?" My voice cracked with the question.

"Nothing. A therapist once told me it's a coping mechanism. I've used it to block the grief I couldn't face. Supposedly, it's not uncommon to block out a chunk of time if there's been tragedy."

I was shaking inside but with great effort I managed to keep my voice calm.

"What happened after they died?"

"I was put up for adoption through a Catholic agency. My parents, Benjamin and Liz Greaves, adopted me. They're good parents. They've provided me with a comfortable life. I don't want to hurt them, which is why I haven't done this sooner, but I want those years back, that time that's just mine. I'm almost thirty years old. I can't protect my parents anymore. I know this will hurt them, my mother especially. She hasn't spoken to me since I told her I was going to do this, but it's something I have to do. I want to have memories like everyone else has. I want to know things about who I was as a little girl, about how I lived, about who loved me. I want to remember those things," she said, the urgency apparent in her tone.

"There's probably a good reason why you blocked it all out," I said quietly.

"I know there was. I know there was a reason then. The four-year-old had to block it all out, or she probably couldn't have lived. Intellectually, I know all that. But I also know that I've stayed busy to avoid having to deal with any of this. I see glimpses of my grief, and I instantly cheer myself up. I can't keep doing that. I can't stay busy the rest of my life.

"I've been in therapy for three years. I've spent eight thousand dollars and hundreds of hours trying to heal myself, and I am sick of sickness and tired of healing. Everyone I know is in therapy, and no one's getting out. I need to do something different. I know what you're trying to say to me, and you're not the first person who's tried to warn me. But I also know that the twenty-nine-year-old woman can probably handle it."

"Probably?" I raised my left eyebrow.

"Will handle it!" she fired back, showing a spark of the feisty survivor she must have been. "Will you help me or not?" she asked defensively, leaning forward to stare at me, almost defying me to say "no."

"I'll help you," I said. The simplicity of my answer seemed to startle her. Frankly, it startled me, too.

"But I have to know something first," I added.

Her suspicion returned. I could see it in her scowl lines.

"Why don't you look yourself?"

She relaxed slightly.

She sat back on the couch and hesitated, almost as if she were carefully choosing her words so I wouldn't change my mind.

"I'm ready to know about the past, Kris, but I'm not ready to deal with all these people in the present. Does that make sense?"

Before I could answer, she continued, "I want you to talk to people about Barbara and Peter Kenwood. I want you to talk to people who knew them and who knew me. I'm ready for that. I'm ready to find out more about the little girl I was. But I still need some distance from it. I'm not ready to try and relate to all these people as an adult, to hear them describe my life as a child. I need the space to process all of this in my own way. Someone like Michelle would probably just run out there and call all these people, invite them over for coffee and have the time of her life."

I smiled in agreement.

"But I'm not Michelle. I'm not like that. It's taken me this long to be able to want to know more. I'm years away from being able to ask the questions myself. That's why I came to see you." She looked toward me for approval.

"One more thing before we start," I said, jumping when a sudden shiver ran through my body, "you'll have to be as honest with me as you can. The more I know about you today, the better I'll be able to understand yesterday. Are you comfortable with that? Do you think we can work together?" My heart beat faster as I waited for her answer.

"I trust you," she replied after only the slightest hesitation.

"Are you sure?"

"There's something about you that's honest. I wouldn't have told you this much if I didn't trust you."

"Okay then, let's get started." I took a legal pad out of my top drawer and prepared to formulate a plan of attack. "Tell me a little about your relationship with your parents, with the parents who adopted you."

"There's not much to tell really. My parents are divorced now. I'm not especially close to either of them, at least not emotionally. But I see them often and we have a decent relationship. My dad's fairly easy-going and aloof."

"And your mom?"

"She's a different story. She's overbearing and controlling, and she's always wanted me to be something more than I am. She does everything in her power to try to make me be what she thinks the ideal daughter is. When I was in college, I started studying English literature because she always wanted to be an English professor. When I fell in love with a woman and changed my major to feminist studies, she threatened to stop paying for college. That made me so mad, I said 'fine'. Instead of confronting her, my father called me at school and told me he'd find a way to get the money to me without my mother knowing. That kind of epitomizes their relationship and the way they communicate. Eventually, my mother came to her senses, and I managed to finish college without laundered money, but I've always felt like I've failed her. Even when I was a little girl, I felt like I wasn't the little girl she wanted."

"What do you mean?"

"I'm not sure really. I just had this vague sense that she wanted me to be different, to be someone else." As she spoke, her tone was neutral, but I could see the sadness in her eyes. Then, as quickly as it came, it passed.

"Can I ask you something, Kris?"

"Sure!"

"It's personal...."

"Okay," I said and cleared my throat.

"Are you in a relationship?"

I hesitated before I answered.

"Do you mean do I have a lover?"

She nodded.

"No, I don't. Why do you ask?"

"I wanted to know something about you, maybe so that it would make it easier for me to tell you about myself, or maybe just because I'm curious."

"I see your point," I paused again, trying to decide exactly how much I would tell her.

"I was in a relationship for three years. It ended a year ago. Her name is Gallagher. She's living in Provincetown now. She says she can't live in the same city with me if we're not in a relationship. I think about her all the time. Now you know something," I said, the pain showing in the strain of my voice.

"Who ended the relationship?"

"I did," I said softly.

"Why? It's obvious you still love her."

"It shows?" I asked, a little embarrassed.

She nodded.

"I do still love her. I just couldn't be in a relationship with her. Intimate relationships are very, very difficult for me. Very difficult," I smiled ruefully.

"Perhaps some day you can tell me about her," Destiny said

16

with more compassion than I'd felt from anyone in a long time.

"Perhaps some day I will. Now can we talk about you, Ms. Greaves?"

"Sure," she said smiling easily.

With that, we made our plans.

I would gather as much information as I could, keeping track of it all, but only revealing it to her a bit at a time, according to how well she was able to handle it.

It all sounded so easy.

As I saw it then, Destiny's case wasn't so much a hunt for her parents as it was for a picture of her family, herself included, reconstructed through others' memories. She never quite stated it this way, but Destiny Greaves wanted me to find her childhood. It sounded easy, but I suspected it would be an awesome task, made bigger by the fact that I knew I'd be hunting for my own childhood as well.

I didn't tell Destiny this, but in agreeing to help her rediscover four lost years of her life, I was also making a commitment to myself.

For, I, too, had no conscious memory, not even fleeting, of my own life before the age of seven.

Before I was done with this case, I would have found parts of Destiny's four years and pieces of my own seven.

Both of our lives would be shattered.

CHAPTER

3

After Destiny left, I walked back to the graphic arts department and looked for my sister Ann who worked for me as an art director. People always commented on how surprising it was that we could work together, and when they found out I was the boss, they always assumed incorrectly that I was the older one. We sounded exactly the same on the phone, which often confused clients and vendors, but in person, we were nothing alike.

For starters, we didn't look alike. We were both about the same medium height and build, with large breasts and small buttocks, but where Ann was soft, I was lean. Ann constantly poofed up her dark brown hair (she'd discovered that if she went to sleep with it wet, she didn't have to pay for as many perms). I wore my light brown, thick, wavy hair in a simple "wash and wear" cut (I'd never had a perm in my life and had no plans for one).

We also didn't dress alike. Ann wore elaborate mix and match outfits in muted colors, dresses that clung to her and panty hose that were every color but tan. I wore what she called my "uniform." A brightly colored, starched button-down shirt, lean cut faded blue jeans (I had ten pairs to choose from), and Topsiders with no socks. I'd improved my whole look several years back when Gallagher taught me to take my crumpled shirts to the dry cleaners.

I found Ann hunched over a drawing board, trying to paste up illustrations of teeth in various stages of gum disease.

She welcomed the interruption.

I asked her to go out to dinner with me that night. She agreed to accompany me if I would treat or give her an advance on her paycheck.

I treated.

Over chips and salsa at our favorite Mexican restaurant, I told her Destiny's story. She agreed it was a fascinating tale and a great case for me to tackle. She also agreed, as she had so many times in the past, to take on added responsibility at the office while I gathered my information.

That taken care of, we got down to the real point of why I'd asked her to dinner.

"I have no memory either, Ann."

"I know, Kris. Frankly, I can't remember much about our childhood myself. And it's probably just as well. From what I do remember, it wasn't such a great time," she said, loudly chomping down on a chip.

"But I want to remember!"

"I know you do. You've tried to remember before and you can't. Years ago, you even talked about hypnosis. Remember when you saw that hypnotherapist on TV, you wanted to go to her."

"I'd forgotten about that. Why didn't I go?"

"She was arrested for fraud a week later."

"Oh, yeah." I laughed. "Just as well."

"Anyway, Kris, I thought you didn't care anymore. I thought you'd let go of it."

"So did I."

She waited for me to continue, maybe because her mouth was full of tortilla chips.

"But when I heard this woman's terrible story, something in me shifted. It was weird. The instant she said she had memory loss, I felt kind of sick inside, but I also knew I could help her get back her memory —"

"Good, that's what she hired you to do."

Ann had a bad habit of interrupting.

"— and I knew I'd get back my own. I knew it, Ann. I've never felt anything like it before. Like I said, it was weird."

"It sounds weird," she said a bit judgmentally for someone who believed more strongly in intuition than logic.

"Do you think I'm ready to remember?"

"I don't know," she said, shaking her head in disapproval. "What's changed? Why now?"

"What's changed, is me. I think I'm stronger now. I've been afraid of delving too deeply into this family stuff, afraid of what I'd find out, afraid of falling apart, of staying in bed, of never coming into work and losing the business. At one time, I was afraid of losing Gallagher. Sure enough, I did. What more do I have to lose now?"

"You'd never stay in bed like she did," Ann said, referring to our mother, who had spent more days in her bed than out of it.

"I know that now, but I haven't always known it. Gallagher and Marketing Consultants were all I had. I couldn't risk it."

"You'd hardly want to lose your business now," she said, and for a split second, I wondered if she was more concerned about me or her job.

"But I wouldn't now," I protested. "That's what I'm telling you. I think I'm strong enough to remember, without it ruining my life. And hell, maybe it will improve things a little."

Maybe I'll be able to sustain an intimate relationship. Maybe I won't start to cough and almost gag when memories I can't grasp fly through my mind. These things, I thought but couldn't say to my sister.

"How will you remember?" She looked at me sharply.

"I'm not sure exactly. By relaxing, I guess. It's all there, like in a computer. We never permanently forget anything. We just lose access to it. This may sound funny, but I'm going to give myself permission to access it."

"That's it?"

"That's it!"

"But you always have a plan, Kris. This isn't like you."

"I know," I said quietly. And despite my resolve, my stomach fluttered. "That's it."

"What about Destiny, how will you help her?"

"Tomorrow afternoon, I start by visiting her father. She called him, and he agreed to meet with me."

"Are you going to meet with her mother, too?"

"No, not yet. She and Destiny aren't getting along too well right now. Also, the two of them never talked about her parents. Destiny's father told her what little she knows and, up until now, she's never had the courage to ask more."

"So she hired you to ask the questions for her," Ann said more as a statement than a question.

"Exactly. She's ready for the information, but she wants some distance from it, too. I can see her point."

"Too bad you can't hire someone to look for your past while you're looking for hers," she kidded.

"Truly!" I said seriously.

"What's she like, this Destiny?"

"She's incredible, very powerful. I like her, which surprises me. She's the first woman Michelle's dated that I genuinely like. The others, I've tolerated, but Destiny's different. She's an amazing woman, especially given the losses she's had in her life. Or maybe because of them."

"Do they go together?"

"Her and Michelle?"

Ann nodded.

"Not hardly! They're so different. Destiny seems so independent, so sure of herself. And Michelle... well, you know Michelle."

"I do!" We both laughed.

"To be fair, though, I haven't actually seen them in the same room yet. I'll be curious to see what they're like as a couple."

The waiter came just then to take our order. After he left, we both were silent for a moment, caught up in our own thoughts.

"You can talk to me if you need to, Kris. I grew up in the same house, you know."

"I know, Ann. Thanks," I said, wishing I could but knowing I couldn't.

• • •

That night, in my apartment in the sky, I thought about my life and why I'd decided to take on Destiny's case. More than for any other reason, I think I'd agreed to help her so that I could come to some sort of peace with my own childhood, which had definitely not been a happy one.

What had my parents done? Perhaps their failings were no more serious than those of two people struggling to raise five children when they were barely able to take care of themselves, but to me, they seemed like atrocities.

Bill and Carolyn Ashe. Their sins began when they married but never fell in love. He was back from the Navy, she was nearing the old-maid age, and their families were from the same Catholic parish. Reasons enough for matrimony. If they didn't love each other, at least their backgrounds were alike. He became an architect. She taught school for one year and then spent the next twenty raising children and resenting the loss of her career.

They were married August 1, 1957. Within days of the ceremony, my mom was pregnant. Ann was born the following May. Gail came one year and one day after that. I was born seventeen months after her. David arrived three years after me.

Adding it all up, by the time my mother was my age, twenty-nine, she had four children, ages six, five, four and one. For a woman who never liked children, much less loved them, she was under severe stress. But she was also Catholic. God forbid she should have exercised her right over the pope's to control her own body.

Four years later, a fifth child was born and somehow, that was the beginning of the end. Capping off nine months of a difficult pregnancy and acute depression was the birth of my sister Jill.

By all accounts, that's when my mother started to go crazy.

She took to her bed for days on end and didn't come out for years. My father held a steady, professional job, golfed every chance he got, and without fail, drank four beers a night. We children ran the house and raised ourselves.

As I lay in bed, I remembered the effect my mother's depression had on me. I remembered walking home from school every day in the third grade, looking up to her bedroom window (for as long as any of us could recall, my mother and father had separate bedrooms). Open curtains meant she was up and about, maybe even acting normal that day. Drawn curtains meant she was still in bed. Maybe we'd eat dinner that night. Maybe we wouldn't. Maybe she'd speak to us. Maybe she wouldn't.

I remembered the Pepsis she drank and the cigarettes she smoked. Most of all, I remembered the way she looked after lying in bed for a week.

I remembered all the years she'd held the family hostage with her moods and her depression. I remembered fearing her and hating her. I never remembered loving her or being loved by her.

As for my father, I remembered he was an alcoholic, though no one dared call him that because he only drank beer and never got drunk. I remembered all the times he'd sent me to the garage. That's where we children ate if we smarted off at the dinner table. I'd spent many nights sitting next to the station wagon, wearing my purple parka, watching the blackened clumps of ice slowly melt away from the tires, trying not to breathe exhaust fumes as I chewed my food.

But I also remembered another side of him. I still had a book he'd given me when I was eight, *What Every Woman Should Know About Football,* the inscription inside alluding to better times, "Love, Mommy and Daddy."

Thoughts of my family kept me awake for hours, but when I finally did sleep, I dreamed about loving a child.

I got out of bed wondering what it would have been like to raise myself. On my way to work, I realized maybe I'd have the chance.

CHAPTER

4

My dream prompted me to make a call when I got to work. I rang Peggy Wood, who had worked for me years ago as a copywriter, and asked her if I could see Zeb and Jessica. It had been more than a year since I'd seen her six-year-old son and four-year-old daughter.

Waking up that morning, I'd realized how much I missed them.

With Peggy's permission, I arranged to take them to the zoo the next day. They were ecstatic. I could hear their childish enthusiasm across the phone lines and it infected me. I hung up the phone feeling lighter than I'd felt in a long time.

I spent the rest of the morning preparing for my appointment with Benjamin Greaves. I made a list of questions to ask him. I combed my hair, trying to make it look like I didn't need a haircut. I dug my leather briefcase out of the storage closet. When all of this was done, I was ready for the first step in my search for Destiny's childhood.

• • •

I drove the short distance from my comfortable, informal office to his high-priced, contemporary office in a glass tower in the center of downtown. When I got off the elevator on the thirty-fifth floor of the Downtown Plaza Building, I was surprised to discover Greaves and Associates, Certified Public Accountants, occupied the entire floor.

I was led to the big man's office by a receptionist who looked bored with her job and my presence. Once there, I was met by another woman who introduced herself as "Mr. Greaves' secretary." She never did tell me her name. Instead, she offered me something to drink. I think she meant coffee or tea. I suggested Coke. She frowned but came back shortly with a can of the real thing and a glass of ice. Before long, I was escorted into the president's office.

Benjamin Greaves greeted me warmly, as if we were old friends. He strode across the room and took my extended hand into both of his. He offered me a seat on one of the three couches in the room and then, instead of returning to the imposing seat behind his desk ten feet away, he positioned himself across from me in a comfortable, overstuffed chair. When he sat, his pot belly easily filled his lap. His thick black hair was parted on the side and graying at the temples. Bushy eyebrows dwarfed his blue eyes.

From my briefcase, I pulled a tiny tape recorder.

"Will Destiny be listening to this?" he asked as I inserted a fresh tape into the recorder.

"She might be. For now, I'm just gathering information and summarizing it for her. At some point, she might want to sift through it all. That's why I'll be taping everything — to make sure she can if she wants to."

"Fair enough," he said easily.

"Ready to go?" I pushed the record button.

"Before we start, Kristin, if you don't mind, could I ask you a few questions?"

"Sure."

"What exactly *is* your relationship with my daughter?"

"What do you mean?" Self-consciously, I glanced at the tape recorder. What had Destiny told him about me? How could I answer that question without giving him an answer?

"Are you special friends?" He looked at me quizzically.

"Oh, no!" I said truthfully. "Nothing like that."

"I wish Destiny could find a nice girl to love. Excuse my boldness, but you seem like a nice girl." He smiled at me.

I started to smile back but then caught myself. This man was smooth. I'd have to watch it or the tape would run out and there would be nothing about the past on it and everything about the present.

It also bothered me that I couldn't get a read on him. I couldn't tell if he was trying to put me at ease, or if he was trying to distract me from the task at hand.

I could have told him the truth about me and Destiny, that we'd only met yesterday, that she'd hired me to investigate her past, that she was dating my friend Michelle, but I didn't. Frankly, I thought the truth was too intimidating. For a moment, I wished that Destiny and I genuinely were friends and that she wasn't my client.

"We're good friends," I said without blinking, and he seemed to accept that.

Before he could think of another question, I blurted out one of my own.

"What exactly has Destiny told you about what I'm doing?"

"She told me you'd be coming here to ask questions about her natural parents."

"Mmm."

"She also instructed me to tell you everything I know. She was quite adamant about that."

"How do you feel about her instructions?"

He didn't reply at once. I watched him pick his words, almost one by one.

"I'm relieved she wants to know, I suppose. I've often wondered why she didn't come to me sooner. For a time, I was even disturbed by her apparent lack of interest in these people who cared for her the first four years of her life. It didn't seem normal."

"What's normal for a young girl who loses both her parents when she's only four years old?" I blurted out, surprising myself with the harshness of my tone.

Destiny's father didn't seem taken aback by my forcefulness.

"You have a point there," he said equably. "I suppose that's why I never pushed her. I hoped she'd come to me someday...."

He paused, a faraway look in his eyes.

"To be candid, Kristin, I never would have imagined she'd send someone in her place. It's odd. We're quite close, closer than most fathers and daughters, I'd venture to say. It's strange she didn't come to me herself. I can't quite understand her motivations."

"Even if you don't understand her, Mr. Greaves, try not to judge her," I said gently. "It took a lot of courage for her to come this far. It's not for us to say if this is far enough."

He looked at me sharply, then softened his features.

"You're right again, young lady. How can I help you... or help Destiny?"

He shifted back in his chair, extended his long legs and put his feet up on the coffee table in front of him. His left foot covered *Business Week*, his right foot covered *Fortune*. I was starting to like him. I took the liberty of matching his pose and put both my feet on President Bush's face, which was disgracing the cover of *Newsweek*.

"Tell me about how you and your wife came to adopt Destiny."

"Let's see... I met Destiny's mother, Liz, when we were seniors at the University of Denver. After we graduated, she went off to Europe for a year — her parents' graduation present to her. Shortly after she returned, we were married."

"Were you in love?"

He intently studied the pattern on his tie. Finally, he looked up and spoke.

"I suppose we were before Liz went to Europe. When she was gone, to occupy my time, I took a few other girls on dates, but nothing serious. When Liz came back, I wouldn't say we were in love, but we did feel a great deal of affection for one another. After her return, our relationship was strained at first. She seemed different, quite a bit more mature, as if she'd aged ten years instead of one. I always suspected she had an affair with a man in Europe, but she never told me about her year away and I never asked."

"How old were you when you got married?"

"We were both twenty-four." He paused. "We honored our wedding vows for almost twenty-five years. Then one day, she asked for a divorce and I granted it. It was quite civil, a formality almost."

"Tell me about Destiny — when did you decide to adopt a child?"

"For several years after we got married, we tried to have a child of our own — without success. When we finally faced the fact that we couldn't have children, Liz insisted we adopt. She was quite anxious to be a mother."

"Er, what prevented you from having children?" I delicately posed the question, hoping for a discreet answer. The gentleman didn't disappoint me.

"I don't know exactly. I suspected something was wrong with Liz's, ahm, workings. I never knew for sure, though. In those days, there weren't the tests available that there are today. Also, I don't think either of us wanted to know for certain. Too much finger-pointing, you know. Even then, Liz and I had an uncanny knack for using that sort of thing against one another."

I saw his point.

"I didn't realize this until years later, but the more we began to realize we couldn't have a child, the more we wanted to have one. We were both quite accustomed to getting our way in the world. We saw this — our barrenness — as an insult."

How bizarre! I wasn't sure Destiny would ever be ready to hear what was on this tape.

"But we also saw it as a challenge, and we set out to adopt a child."

"How did you go about that?"

"Privately. If you've been around the block even once, you'll find the private sector always operates more efficiently than the public one."

Remembering my last trip to the post office, I nodded in agreement.

"It was set up through our church, Church of Christ."

"A Catholic church?"

"Yes. At the time, Liz and I were both practicing Catholics. We raised Destiny as a Catholic."

Poor Destiny.

"By the time we finally put our name on a waiting list, they told us it would be two or three years before we'd get a healthy, Caucasian infant."

"Did you want an infant?"

"I did initially. I don't know if Liz did, but she went crazy when she heard how long we'd have to wait. As I said, the more times we, er, had relations without conceiving, the more desperate she became."

"You couldn't wait a couple of years?"

"No, we couldn't. We wanted to get on with the business of having a family. I was a practical man. I couldn't give a home to a child who wasn't Caucasian. Liz couldn't provide care for a child who was ill. We both knew that much about ourselves. As I said, I was practical. Older children needed homes, too. I was content to settle for an older child. Liz agreed, although she insisted the child be a girl."

He must have seen me flinch at the word "settle."

"I know what I just said sounds a bit callous, but it's how I felt.

29

Having a child of our own was my first choice. Adopting an infant was my second choice. However, we can't always have our first choices in life, and rightly so. My third choice, Destiny, has given me more joy than any other person in my life," he said and I knew he meant it.

"Do you have any regrets about not having children of your own or not adopting an infant?"

"Not in the least. I've adored Destiny from the moment I set eyes on her," he said with more love than I'd ever felt from either of my own parents.

"How did you come to adopt her, specifically?"

"Six months after we put our names on the waiting list, we got a call. A four-year-old girl was available. Her parents, who lived in a parish across town, had died in a car crash. At the time, that parish, St. Peter's, was comprised of mostly elderly people. Their first choice — you see, Kristin, first choices rarely come to fruition, even for the church — had been to place Destiny in a family in their own parish. Fortunately for us, no qualified families came forward to claim her."

He paused again.

"I remember the nun telling me on the phone that she had blonde hair. That did it for me. I always wanted to marry a girl with golden locks."

"What color is Mrs. Greaves' hair?" I asked, curious to see if he'd gotten his first choice.

"Dark brown. At any rate, it was the last time I saw her, but she's been known to color her hair."

"Has she ever been a blonde?" I asked playfully.

"No, damn it!" We both laughed.

"What did Destiny look like when she first came to you?"

"Oh, she was beautiful. Like an angel."

"Was she scared?"

"If she was, she didn't show it. I think Liz and I and the nuns who brought her were more nervous than she was," he chuckled.

"Was she aware of her parents' death?"

"Oh yes." He nodded vehemently. "She was extremely sad. She would never cry in front of us but she was sad. You could see it in her eyes. She fully understood her loss, I'm convinced of it. The nun who brought her told us she was too young to comprehend what had happened to her, but I always thought she knew. She was grieving. Not like we adults grieve. That's why most people couldn't see it in her. But she grieved. No doubt about it."

"How did she grieve?"

"You could see the sadness in her. She went through all the stages of grief, like a four-year-old adult: anger, denial, finally, acceptance. When she first came to us, she cried herself to sleep every night. Countless times, I'd hear her sobbing, grief wracking her tiny body, and I'd go to her room to comfort her. Except she couldn't accept my comfort — or Liz's either. The minute she saw us, she'd stop crying. Just like that, her tears would dry up." He snapped his fingers to accent his point.

"Most children cry for attention. Destiny cried only for herself. I tried to talk to her, to tell her it was appropriate for her to cry, appropriate for her to share her sadness with us, but she never responded. Liz called her 'the little warrior,' in anger I suppose, because this tiny human being wouldn't — couldn't — accept her as a replacement for her mother. To this day, I'm not sure Destiny accepts Liz as her mother. It's uncanny — they even look a bit alike, but they're as different as night and day. Liz tried to be the perfect mother for Destiny. No one can fault her for trying, but I don't think Liz ever was able to give Destiny what she needed. Nor was I, for that matter."

"Those first months must have been hard for you."

He stopped for a moment to consider my sympathy.

"It was rather tense," he said. "The nuns told us there would be a period of adjustment. It was awkward for all of us. For Liz and myself as instant parents and for Destiny who had lost a family and gained one — in less than a month."

"How long did it take you to adjust to each other?"

"Oh, it was a good year, maybe more. I can't point to a moment in time when things changed, but eventually they did."

He paused.

"Come to think of it, I do remember one Sunday in particular. Destiny and I went to the playground — this must have been almost a year and a half after we got her — and from a distance, I watched Destiny play with the other children. She and two other girls were swinging, and for the first time I saw her true spunk. She was pumping her little legs so hard, I thought she'd touch the sky. I saw a spark in her then, that same spark she has today that drives me crazy, and I knew she'd come back to life. It was frightening really, because I also realized how dead she must have been. Contrasting her two personalities, she'd come to us not much caring whether she lived or died. That day, on the playground, I saw how much she wanted to live."

He gave me a half-smile.

"When the people from the church first told us about Destiny, they all told us how resilient children are. I think they were afraid to acknowledge how much pain there could be in one so young."

"Why didn't someone in her own family, someone related to the Kenwoods, adopt her?"

"I'm not sure, but I don't think there was anyone. The nuns told us there was a grandmother she was close to — the father's mother, I believe — but she was in her fifties and a bit sick, if I remember correctly. There was no other family from what I was led to believe, but we weren't told much. Destiny came to us with the clothes on her back, nothing more."

"Nothing?" I was incredulous. "Not even toys or photographs or anything?"

"Nothing. The nuns thought it was better that way — that she leave her old life behind and start a completely new one."

"My God!"

"It was sad," he said. "A very difficult time."

"Is the grandmother still alive?"

"I would presume so."

"What's her name?"

He hesitated before answering me.

"I'm not sure Destiny should contact her."

"Why not?"

"It might be difficult for her, coming face-to-face with someone she hasn't seen in twenty-five years. It might bring back her grief."

"And it might help heal her."

"Perhaps," he said without conviction. "Are you a parent?"

"No," I said, startled by his question.

"Then you can't know what it's like to try to protect a child. I don't want Destiny to grieve anymore. I saw her grieve once. Once was enough, don't you think?"

I didn't see any point in debating, but I answered his question in my mind. Once was enough if Destiny said it was enough. If she had more grieving to do, she'd do it. I could see the toll her grief had already taken on Benjamin Greaves, but I couldn't let that stop me. I had a job to do, for Destiny and for myself, and I would do it.

Regardless the price. Regardless the pain.

Out loud, I asked again, "I would appreciate it if you would give me her name."

"Kenwood, Marie Kenwood," he said, looking tired. "Last I knew, she lived somewhere in southeast Denver."

"Thank you."

We finished up then. I turned off the tape recorder. I asked if I could return for more information if I needed it at a later date. He said I could. We shook hands, as if we'd just conducted a satisfying piece of business. As I was walking out of his office, I wondered if he'd sleep well that night.

I know now that there's no way he would have gotten a wink of sleep if he'd had any idea what he'd started. It didn't seem like much at the time, but the information he'd given me, sometimes willingly, sometimes not, was to lead to drastic discoveries in his daughter's life... and in his own.

CHAPTER

5

When I got back to my office, I called Destiny and summarized my meeting with her father. I left out all the emotion, all the description of her life as a four-year-old, and got straight to the point.

"You may have a grandmother living in Denver, Peter Kenwood's mother. Do you want me to find her?"

"My father told you that?" Her voice registered both shock and fear.

"Yes."

"How does he know about her. What does he know about her? Why haven't I heard about her before now?" she cried.

"He doesn't know much about her, just what little the nuns told him at the time, which believe me, wasn't very much. It seems the church was very concerned with there being as little connection as possible between your old life and your new life. For *your* sake, they said."

"Right," she said angrily.

"Nothing about this is fair, Destiny. Or easy. That much I got, very clearly, in my meeting with your dad. What happened to you is incredibly sad. I know you know that in your head. But now, Destiny, if we follow through with this, you'll know it in your heart. It's not the same thing. What you're doing — what we're doing — is hard."

I waited for her to say something. Silence.

"Are you still there?"

"I'm here," she said, sounding as if she were fighting back tears.

"Do you want me to keep going? Do you want me to try to find this woman?"

"Yes," she said with simple determination.

Her resolve frightened me.

"Okay, then, I'll let you know when I find her. But don't hold your breath, Destiny. There's a good chance she's dead. Or senile. If she's alive, she'd have to be well into her eighties. Don't get your hopes up, okay?"

"I never do."

"All right," I let out a sigh, "so I'll look for Marie Kenwood?"

"Yes."

When she agreed, I knew then that she really trusted me. And I was flattered, because the more I found out about her, the more I knew trust couldn't possibly have come easily to this "little warrior."

God help us all, I thought as I opened up the phone book and started to call the Denver-area Kenwoods. God help us all.

• • •

Finding Destiny's grandmother was so easy it startled me. On the third try, I located her. Marie Kenwood was very alive, very lucid, and very suspicious of me. It took every ounce of charm I had to get her to reluctantly agree to meet with me the following week.

I left work that evening feeling like I'd accomplished quite a lot for one day. Not even the forecast of snow for the following day could dampen my spirits. I felt better than I'd felt in months.

It didn't last long.

Alone, I went to a mindless movie, ate more popcorn and chocolate-covered raisins than I should have, and inched my car home in the driving sleet.

When I got home, I cleared the debris from my bed, and tried to fall asleep.

But I couldn't sleep. I couldn't stop thinking about what Benjamin Greaves had told me.

I thought about what he'd said about Destiny not wanting to cry in front of them. I never cried in front of my parents either. I didn't have a single recollection of my mom comforting me when I cried. Just the opposite, in fact. In my teens, when I fought with her, I would will myself not to cry in front of her. I would focus on something in the room, stare at it and try to keep control of myself because I never wanted to show emotion to her. If she saw me cry, she won. If I held back the tears, I won.

By then, obviously, I didn't trust her with my feelings, but I wondered when that mistrust had started.

I remembered hiding myself from her. When I started menstruating, I threw away my soiled underwear and used Kleenex as Kotex because I didn't know what else to do and was too afraid to talk to her or to my older sisters. When one day after I stood up in front of my entire eighth-grade French class, and a girl I barely knew pulled me aside to tell me blood had soaked through my orange bell-bottoms, I had to call my mom to come get me. On the way home, she told me how surprising it was that my flow was so heavy with my first menstrual cycle. I never bothered to tell her it was actually my sixth one.

When did my own mother become my enemy, so much so that I was afraid to tell her anything?

And where was my father when I was growing up? The memories of him were almost completely blocked. It was as if he didn't exist. Why?

These questions, the questions to which there were no acceptable answers, depressed me until eventually I fell asleep.

I woke up long before morning came, sweating and shaking from a terrifying dream.

Ann and I are walking through the woods at night. In line, Ann is in front, then me. As we go to cross a bridge, I step aside. I won't cross it. I am going to walk parallel to it.

Ann goes on ahead, then disappears, as if into a hole. I scream and scream for her. I am terrified. I keep trying to wake up. In my dream, I remind myself I am in my apartment and safe. I'm calm, then the terror again. I scream louder and louder but never make a sound.

As I remembered pieces of the dream, thoughts flashed through my mind:

Camping trips. We'd taken several family camping trips. My mother never went along because she hated camping. Who slept in the tent with Dad? Who slept in the car? My incomplete thoughts terrified me more than the dream itself.

I started crying from a place I could not touch.

Total amnesia. It could no longer protect me. What would?

Finally, when I could no longer stand the noise inside my

head, I put on my stereo headphones, turned up the music as loud as I could, and read *People* magazine.

For hours, I kept the external noise going to override the internal noise. I was exhausted, yet couldn't chance sleep. Just before dawn, I returned to my bed, lit a candle on the nightstand, and prayed for peace.

Mercifully, the morning finally came, but not soon enough, and not nearly easily enough.

•••

To make a bad night worse, I opened my blinds to a blanket of fresh snow.

On a clear day, from my high-rise windows, I could see two hundred miles of Colorado's majestic Rocky Mountains — from Colorado Springs' Pike's Peak to Boulder's Flatirons. That gray day, however, was an exception. I could barely see the highway, which was only a mile away. Everywhere I looked, the white film covered the cars and streets and buildings below me. Undaunted, I dressed warmly and left to pick up the kids, hoping their youthful energy would erase some of the terror of the night before.

I wasn't disappointed. As soon as I got to their house, Zeb and Jessica piled on me, first hugging me, then wrestling with me. By committee, we decided to go to Funworld Sports Center, saving the zoo for a drier, warmer day.

In the car, Jessica loudly told me she missed me. That it had been eighteen-hundred days since she'd last seen me. I smiled and said I missed her, too. Zeb, in his infinite six-year-old wisdom corrected his four-year-old sister and told her it had only been three hundred days. Surprisingly, he wasn't far off in his calculations.

Jessica, unimpressed by Zeb's correction, squirmed in the back seat and occupied her time by waving at cars. No one in the cars waved back, but that didn't affect her enthusiasm.

In Funworld's parking lot, as I was lifting Jessica out of the back seat, she quietly said to me, "I prayed you would come."

"And I did," was all I could say as I set her on the ground and quickly turned so she wouldn't see my tears. Holding hands, we ran through the parking lot, trying without success to avoid puddles of slush.

Once inside, we played and played. We swam. We drove

bumper cars. We bounced around in a room full of balls. We ate corn dogs and pizza and nachos and french fries. We drank lemonade and Dr. Pepper and milkshakes.

Over lunch, Jessica told me she had two married cats. She knew they were married because one of the cats just had kittens. I marveled at her right-wing, moral logic. Zeb told me his dog Moe had eaten one of his goldfish. After the fish had jumped out of the bowl and hit the floor, he explained with zeal. We laughed and told more stories.

That evening, after I'd taken them back to their home, I cried and cried. Partly, I cried for how much I missed them.

Mostly, I cried for how much I missed myself.

• • •

The next day, which was Sunday, Michelle called to invite me to brunch with her and Destiny. They were going to try a quaint restaurant in Park Hill. I declined. I wanted to see them, but not together, not that day. Maybe not until I was done with Destiny's case, I told her.

She accepted that without argument, probably because Destiny's naked body was lying next to her, I thought wryly. As we were hanging up, she told me she was going to see a psychic to ask her about Destiny's childhood. I heard a giggle in the background. Great. I told her I'd be anxious to hear what the psychic had to say. Michelle coyly suggested she might not share her information with me, or with Destiny either. Another giggle.

Michelle and I set up dinner plans for Friday night, just the two of us, and I put down the phone wondering how Michelle had ever come to be my friend.

• • •

Feeling lonely and faced with an entire empty day ahead of me, I decided to call Grandma Ashe, my father's mother. She was home, as she almost always was, and eagerly accepted when I invited myself over to her house for dinner and cards.

I spent most of that cold, dreary day snacking, napping, reading and watching TV. By late afternoon, I was feeling queasy from having lain around all day.

I summoned enough energy to put on my shorts and head to the racquetball room in the basement of my apartment building.

In an empty court, I volleyed for an hour before I became bored.

I trudged back up to my apartment, took a quick shower, and drove the six blocks to my grandma's house. I would have walked, but there was an ominous chill in the air that night, a bite from which my car only slightly protected me.

Promptly at 6 p.m. (right after Lawrence Welk), we sat down to one of her typical dinners, high in starch and low in imagination: roast beef, noodles, mashed potatoes, rolls. I happily ate everything on my plate and pleased her by taking seconds. After dinner, we cleared the dishes into the sink and retired to the living room.

My grandma had to go to the bathroom, so I got out the card table. Setting it up reminded me of the first time she let me play cards with her lady friends. One of the eight women in her Canasta Club had been sick and, at the age of nine, I was her substitute. I smiled as I remembered how my brash style of play had offended everyone, except my grandma.

Grandma and I were partners and we won all afternoon. Having played cards with me many times before, Grandma wasn't surprised by my reckless strategy, but it sure raised a few other whitish-blue eyebrows. I never played illegally. I simply played like the cocky kid I was. Hand after hand, I went out, ending the game with the ladies holding fists full of cards and mouths full of air. On the rare occasions when I had a bad hand (and sometimes even when I didn't), I'd loudly announce "This isn't a hand, it's a foot!" and Grandma and I would both laugh as if it were the funniest thing we'd ever heard. Despite her friends' scrutiny, my grandmother loved me more than ever that afternoon twenty years ago.

When Grandma emerged from the bathroom, we got down to some serious playing, chatting amiably between discards.

At one point, as I watched her lay down her cards, I thought about all the happy hours I'd spent at her house: baking cookies and eating them fresh from the oven, taking walks in Washington Park, sitting on her glider in the warm summer evenings. My grandma's favorite story, which she told so often I could almost remember it happening, was about how I was the only grandchild she ever had to spank. When I was three years old, she gave me a swat, so soft it couldn't have hurt a flea. I defiantly told her "Didn't hurt!" My gentle grandmother said, "I didn't mean for it to hurt, Kristin," and pulled me into her arms.

Although she was eighty-six and in near perfect health, I

worried about the day I would lose her.

"Do you ever think about dying, Grandma?"

She answered my serious question without missing a beat.

"Only when the mortuary calls," she said matter-of-factly as she laid down a card I wanted.

"They call you?"

"Once a month."

"You're kidding!"

"I'm not. Honey, do you want that ace or not?" she asked. I'd been so shocked by the thought of a mortuary teleprospecting my grandma that I'd forgotten to play.

"Er, yes. I'm going to pick up the pile. What do you tell them?"

"I tell them I'll get back to them when I'm ready."

I tried not to laugh because I thought she was serious.

"Won't it be a little late then?" I asked reasonably.

"Oh, well," she said, laughing mischievously. Once again, she'd fooled me.

We played on, though I'd lost my concentration.

"I do think about what will happen to me," she said.

"When you die?"

"No, if I get sick."

"You don't worry about dying?"

"Not any more."

"You just worry about being alive?"

"Every night, I pray that when I leave this house, it will be feet first."

"Huh," was all I could say, knowing what she meant, but unable to bear the picture of my grandma on a stretcher.

"Everyone I know is dead. Most of my friends are dead or dying. Your grandfather's been dead for forty years. I'm glad I never remarried. I would have had to bury two more."

"You outlived both the men you considered marrying?"

"I did."

"Tell me about them."

She proceeded to tell me the stories I'd already heard but loved to hear over and over again. Tales from her past kept us busy until it was time for me to go.

When she went into the bedroom to retrieve my coat, suddenly I knew it was time.

For a brief moment, I was like a detective working on my own case. Except I wasn't all there. My detached self was working to solve the mystery of what had happened to my emotional self.

41

When Grandma returned, I asked her one question, a question I'd never been able to ask before. One was enough.

"Hey, Grandma, what kind of a father was Dad?"

Instead of answering my question, she posed one of her own. "What do you mean, honey?"

For some reason, my stomach suddenly felt sick. I willed control of my voice and casually said, "Nothing specific, just what kind of a father was he? I can't remember much about when I was really little and I just wondered what he was like."

With that, I fell silent. It took her the longest time to answer. I struggled into my coat as I waited.

"Well," she said, still thinking, "when you girls were young, he liked to bathe you, and diaper you...."

As she continued to speak, I fought to control myself. At the words, "He liked to bathe you," my stomach had dropped and I'd felt the strangest impulse to burst out in laughter — nervous, hysterical peals of mirthless laughter. I needed information, but I couldn't give information. I had to appear calm, almost disinterested.

My grandmother's voice, by now far away, went on.

"...later on, when you got to be older, he didn't take as much of an interest in your lives...."

I didn't hear anything else she said. Not about her son. Not about anything. As quickly as I could, I hugged her tightly, kissed her cheek, and ran out into the night, clutching the leftovers she'd insisted I take for my lunch the next day.

Driving home, the most absurd memory came to me. I remembered the swimming lessons my sisters and I had taken for several summers in a row beginning when we were ages six, five and four. We had all started in the beginning swimming class, and failing to ever advance, had all ended in it. Undaunted, my mother brought us back, time after time, for the next session of beginning swimming. Every single session, all three of us failed.

For two summers, we grew taller and taller, and came back to each new session of the class embarrassed by our height, our age, and our inability to move on. In light of the fact that every single other child in each of our classes passed, my mother couldn't understand our failure. We were all three fit, coordinated children, especially Gail and I. Gail went on to excel at soccer. I played football, tennis, and baseball with the best of the boys. Finally, although she couldn't fathom it, my mother accepted that we would never be able to swim. We were grateful when we didn't have to return for further humiliation.

"My God!" I said out loud as I carefully steered my car on the snow-packed streets, "I was four years old then."

"I was four years old then," I kept repeating over and over again, louder and louder each time until finally it became a high-pitched scream. My first conscious memory, and what a horrible one it was.

"Why couldn't we swim?" I whispered, because my throat hurt from screaming.

Perhaps we were terrified of the water, it occurred to me for the first time in my life. Not for its ripples, but rather for its touches.

I didn't sleep well that night.

Someone is attacking me. The person crawls into my bed and snuggles against me, flesh completely covering my little body, hands clutching my sleeper pajamas. I see my attacker's hands. They remind me of someone, but I cannot think who.

44

CHAPTER

6

The next day at work, I sluggishly went through my paces. I rewrote an article, "Ten Steps To A More Relaxed Pap Smear." I called a few of my clients. I chatted with my employees (carefully avoiding time alone with Ann). Nothing spectacular, but it sure beat thinking about the past — mine or Destiny's.

The next few days were much the same until Wednesday when I left work early to meet Marie Kenwood.

I drove east for what seemed like forever until finally, at the southeast edge of Denver, I found my turn-off.

Marie Kenwood lived in a moderately-priced retirement community, one of those "planned neighborhoods" that has plenty of green beltways, few amenities and the appearance of security. Inside her complex, the streets meandered in every direction but a sensible one, and it was almost impossible to distinguish one residence from another. Even with the oversized address numbers and the color-coordinated blocks, it wouldn't have surprised me if half the residents had, at some point, tried to enter another person's house.

Twice, I drove past the golf course, totally lost. Finally, at wit's end, I stopped in at the clubhouse to ask directions. An elderly man told me he was going my way and offered to let me follow him. At a snail's pace, I followed his blue Pontiac to Mrs. Kenwood's doorstep. As he drove off, I waved my thanks; he tipped his hat.

I rang the bell and waited anxiously for Mrs. Kenwood. When

45

at last she opened the door, I let out a sigh of relief. I think I had been afraid she'd be as intimidating in person as she'd been on the phone.

But how could she intimidate me? I towered over her, not because I'm extraordinarily tall, but because my 5'6" were giant next to her 4'10" (including stacked-up hair).

My relief came too soon.

"Mrs. Kenwood?" I asked politely as I extended my hand.

"Of course I am, young lady," she said, ignoring my outstretched hand. "Come in out of the cold." She directed me past her into the foyer. I turned back to her, once again attempting to introduce myself.

"I'm Kristin Ashe. I'm pleased to —" I didn't have a chance to finish my greeting.

"Of course you are. You're late," she said, deliberately looking at the elegant lady's pocket watch hanging from a gold chain around her neck. "Six minutes late, to be exact."

"Er, yes," I said apologetically. "I would have been early, but I got turned around in the complex. Some kind gentleman helped me find —"

"Never mind," she barked. "You're here now. Would you like some tea?" she asked, sounding more like a platoon leader than a hostess.

I hated tea but I didn't dare ask for Dr. Pepper.

"Yes, please."

"Fine, then. Have a seat. I'll be back shortly."

She ushered me into the living room and disappeared around the corner. Delicately, I sat down on one end of her flowered couch, hugging the armrest for support, somehow fearing she'd burst into the room and claim I was sitting in her seat. Timidly, ever conscious of her nearby presence, I looked around me.

On every wall, there was a painting. Of mountain scenes. Of ocean scenes. Of trains. Of flowers. Each one was recognizable for what the artist had tried to paint, but that was the extent of the talent.

Her coffee table overflowed with magazines and newspapers. *Catholic Register. Good Housekeeping. Ladies Home Journal. Farmer's Almanac.* Nothing I wanted to read.

On the floor next to the couch, a large cotton bag held yarn and knitting needles. Straight ahead sat a television set. I glanced around the room and dread filled me as I realized I was sitting in the place that had the best view of the TV. That, combined with the bag, convinced me I was sitting in Mrs. Kenwood's favorite spot. I quickly scurried down to the other end of the couch.

And not a moment too soon. I had barely jumped up from her cherished seat when she came through the doorway carrying a silver tray. She set it on the coffee table in front of the couch and then sat in the exact spot I'd just occupied.

"Here it is," she said, almost begrudgingly.

"Thank you. And thanks for agreeing to meet with me," I said, reaching for a cup and saucer after it became clear she wasn't going to serve me. I raised the cup to my mouth, ready to take my first sip.

"This isn't a tea party. I'm a busy woman, Miss Ashe. I expect you'll be brief," she started in as I innocently blew on the tea.

"Of course," I said, setting my cup down, a little miffed. First, she had just about demanded I take the tea. Then, she had practically ordered me not to drink it.

"You agreed to talk with me for an hour. I'll respect that," I said, wondering how I'd gotten her to agree to anything. Obviously, she resented my intrusion in her staid life.

I'd been up front with Benjamin Greaves about taping our conversation. I'd intended to be honest with Marie Kenwood, too, but seeing how cantankerous she was, I opted for deception. I reached into my pocket, turned on the tiny tape recorder and pulled out a Kleenex. I wiped my dry nose as the older woman again looked at her watch and deliberately avoided my gaze.

Ignoring my tea, I relaxed back into the couch, shifted my body so that it was facing her, flashed my brightest smile and said, "So tell me about Destiny, Mrs. Kenwood."

For the first time, she looked directly at me.

"Are your eyeglasses purple and red?" she asked as she squinted and leaned forward for a better look.

"Yes," I said wearily, preparing for a lecture.

"I like colorful things," she said, totally surprising me.

Well, that was all the encouragement I needed. Her cold veneer had slipped for an instant. Shamelessly, I took full advantage of the moment.

"You must. The artwork on your walls is beautiful," I said, lying without a trace of guilt.

"Oh, those, they're nothing. Just a little something I did in my painting class." She smiled for the first time.

"You painted them?" I feigned surprise.

"I certainly did."

"You're quite talented. I especially like the one of the sea. The colors are extraordinary."

That must have been enough flattery for her because she changed the subject.

"So you want to know about Destiny, eh? After all these years, you come into my life to ask me about Destiny?" She pushed her eyeglasses up her nose.

"Er, yes." I felt so timid around her.

"Before you called, young lady, I hadn't heard that name for some time. After my son Peter died, after the little one left, I forbade people to utter their names."

"I'm sorry for your loss, Mrs. Kenwood," I said, meaning the loss of her son.

"I missed her every day, you know. No one ever thought about that when they took her away," she said with more than a trace of bitterness.

"Why didn't you ever see her?"

"The Sisters wouldn't allow it. They found her a new family, and they came to get her. It was best for her, they said, best for the child."

"Were the two of you close?"

"And how! I was her Nana — that was what she called me. Barbara was forever trying to get her to call me Grandma Kenwood, but she never would," the older woman said with a hint of triumph. "She was such a beautiful child," she added, almost as an afterthought.

"She's quite beautiful now," I said softly, but I don't think she heard me.

"She was never more beautiful than the night her father died. We were together, you know. The kids had dropped her off earlier in the evening. What a grand evening that was."

I wasn't sure I'd heard her right.

"Pardon me?"

"Oh yes," she said, startled by my voice. "It was a grand evening. We made sugar cookies and paper dolls. Destiny took a bubble bath. We overflowed the tub with bubbles and laughed at our silliness. I tucked her into bed. She was so tired — as only the young can get. I think she was asleep before her head hit the pillow. I kissed her forehead and turned out the light." All of this Marie Kenwood said, as if reciting a poem.

"That was our last happy time," she continued. "I was still up, reading, when the phone call came. My boy was dead."

She pulled a tissue out of her sleeve and dabbed at her eyes.

"They didn't tell me then, on that awful night, that I'd lose Destiny, too, but I knew it." She paused. "I knew they'd take her away from me."

"That night, did you tell Destiny her parents had, ahm, passed away?"

"Dead is the word, young lady. They weren't passed away. They were dead," she said, the fatigue evident in her voice. "Someone had to do it, so yes, I told Destiny, but not that night. For six and a half hours, I cried in the dark. I thought the sun would never come up again. When it did, I told her."

"What did you tell her?"

"Oh, my, I can hardly remember. I tried to compose myself before I woke her. No sense letting her see her Nana cry. If I recall correctly, I told her that her parents were in heaven with Baby Jesus. That made her happy. Then I told her the truth, that she wouldn't be seeing them anymore. At that, she started crying... and I started crying again, too, a little."

"I couldn't help myself," she added, as if she owed me an explanation. "I remember, she patted me on the head and said, 'It's okay, Nana.' "

"Did you ever think of being Destiny's guardian?"

"Of course, I did," she said spiritedly. "But do you think they'd award custody to a 57-year-old widow with diabetes just because it made the most sense? Of course not! I was all alone. My husband, Rudy, had died of cancer the year before. Unfit, the nuns told me. As if they knew what was best for my Destiny."

"Weren't there any other family members who could have taken custody?"

"I was her only family on Peter's side. He was our only child. On Barbara's side, there was her parents and a sister, but they lived back East and hadn't seen the child but once or twice. They didn't care a whit about her," she said with disgust.

"Barbara wasn't close to her family?"

"No, siree. They cut her off when she married our Peter. They saw her a few times after the child was born, but that was it. They never even came to the funeral. Imagine that — wouldn't come to Colorado to bury their own daughter."

"Why didn't they like Peter?"

"He wasn't rich enough for the likes of them. They wanted Barbara to marry some society boy. She went against them when she fell in love with Peter. Rudy always said she was better off not talking to them, but I don't think it's natural when parents don't have relations with their children."

"Were Barbara and Peter in love?"

"Oh, my, yes! 'Til the day they died, they were in love. You'd never seen two kids as in love as they were. Made you uncomfortable sometimes." She chuckled at the memory.

"How did they meet?"

"They met at school, that school in Fort Collins. He was studying to be a high school teacher. She wanted to be a nurse. They were married in '52, but I can't remember the exact day any more. I never was good at remembering dates. Rudy would remember if he was here. That man could remember everything. Some things were better off not remembered, I'd tell him, but he'd insist on remembering, the stubborn old fool," she said affectionately.

"It sounds like you loved Rudy quite a lot."

"We were suited for each other."

"This may be a hard question for you to answer, Mrs. Kenwood, but I have to ask it —"

"Don't coddle me, young lady. Nothing's too hard when you've lived through eight decades. Ask your question!"

"Okay," I swallowed hard. "How did you ever manage to say good-bye to Destiny? How could you say good-bye to her when you knew you'd never see her again?"

She fiddled with her dress, ironing out every invisible wrinkle, before she answered me.

"First of all, I thought I'd see her again. I didn't know when, but I was led to believe I could stay in touch. It wasn't until after they'd taken her away that the Sisters phoned me and told me I shouldn't ever contact her."

She took a sip of her tea, which must have been stone cold. She showed no sign of noticing.

"I remember the day they came to get her. She had been staying with me while the church looked for a suitable family. I was a fit guardian for a month, you see, but no more. Secretly, I think they were afraid I'd die before she graduated from high school. Well, I've shown them a thing or two, now, haven't I?"

She tried to suppress a cough.

"Heavens, that must have been the coldest day of that winter. I know because my pipes froze up that night. I had the child bundled up as I'd always done when I was sending her home with

Peter. The only thing showing on her was her big, green saucer eyes. The rest of her was clothes. When I heard the doorbell, we said our good-byes. I'd already explained all the rest to her, so we were ready. I'd told her she was going to get a new family, a new house, new friends, and that she'd be very happy. I'd told her she'd get new toys, but even that didn't cheer her up. She was very down that day.

"In the middle of me telling her this, she interrupted me — I never could teach her to stop interrupting with her infernal questions — and asked, 'Will I ever see you again, Nana?' Well, what could I say to the child? I couldn't lie to her and I couldn't tell her the truth. I did the best thing I could think of. I said, 'Yes, Destiny, you will. Someday soon, you will, but now you have to go live with your new family.' She was a bright child, she always had been, and she knew that someday never comes. She burst into tears. The doorbell rang again, and I didn't know what to do. I tried to comfort her as best I could. I told her not to cry, that everything would be okay, that her new family wouldn't want to see her cry, that I loved her. Then I answered the door and she left with the two Sisters. I went back inside the house, and that was that."

"That must have been hard for you."

"It was," she said simply. Right then, she noticed I hadn't drunk a sip of my tea. "There, there, let me get you some fresh tea. There's plenty of time for talking."

With that, I knew I had her. We spent the rest of the afternoon talking about Barbara, Peter and Destiny Kenwood and about Marie and Rudy Kenwood. Twice, I had to excuse myself to change tapes in the bathroom. Each time, I felt guilty about taping our conversation without her knowledge, but then I reminded myself that I represented Destiny, not Mrs. Kenwood, and I did it anyway. Had I asked her permission, maybe she would have even said "yes," but I couldn't quite see Mrs. Kenwood understanding or appreciating the modern tools of technology. She probably would have told me, "If you can't remember it, you don't need to."

I had started out the afternoon afraid of her; I ended it respecting her.

Before I left, she gave me the name and phone number of Barbara's best friend, Lydia Barton. Lydia, who had lived next door to the Kenwoods when Destiny was little, would be able to help me put together more of the pieces. Marie said she'd call to

51

let her know I'd be contacting her.

Interestingly, Marie Kenwood never asked any questions about Destiny Greaves, and I never offered any information. Perhaps too many years had passed for her to let herself care about "the little one" again.

As I was leaving, she did start to ask me something but then caught herself. I encouraged her to tell me what was on her mind, but she wouldn't.

I thanked her profusely for her time and for an enjoyable afternoon. She brushed aside my appreciation and told me to zip up my coat.

After I left, I drove off thinking about all that she'd told me and which pieces of it I'd tell Destiny.

CHAPTER

7

All the next day, with a trace of anxiety, I looked forward to the dinner I'd arranged with Destiny.

When I got to Nadine's Diner a few minutes early, she was already waiting in the lobby. She seemed nervous.

After we were seated and had ordered, I started to tell her about her grandmother. She quickly stopped me.

"Could we just talk awhile, Kris, about anything? Anything except my family. I need a little time."

"Okay," I agreed easily. "What do you want to talk about?"

"How about Kristin Ashe?"

"Very funny." I smiled.

"I'm serious," she said, looking at me intently. "I'm curious about you. You intrigue me."

For a second, I forgot she was dating Michelle.

"Okay," I muttered after I regained my composure. "What do you want to know?"

"For starters, why is a woman as attractive as you not in a relationship?"

I laughed. "It's an anomaly. A brief respite in the universe of time."

She laughed with me but waited for me to say more.

"Actually, this is the first time in my life, since I was eighteen, that I'm not in a relationship. I've never not been in a relationship. Four different women, with very little, if any, time between each one. This last year, since Gallagher left, has been the

53

longest time I've been out of a relationship, and I have to tell you, it's a relief. I'm lonely as hell, but I was usually lonely when I was in a relationship. Frankly, I feel like a burden's been lifted."

"The burden of Gallagher?" She looked right at me, almost into me.

"No, not at all. The burden of being in an intimate relationship. The expectations that go along with the words 'I want to be with you.' It's such a struggle, such an incredible struggle for me to be in relationships with people. Especially my lovers, but not just them. Friendship is hard for me, too; so is relating to my employees."

"Why?"

I had to break eye contact before I could answer. "I don't know why, but the pattern's always the same. I start out trusting people. On a very superficial level, I love them. They fascinate me. I like getting to know them. I start out trusting them, then day by day, I pull back a piece of myself, hoping the other person won't find me out, that they won't know I've checked out, checked back inside myself."

"Michelle's right — we are alike," she said quietly.

"How so," I asked, at once relieved and irritated that she'd broken into my monologue.

"I can't be close to people either, Kris. You've had four long-term relationships. I haven't even had one. I can't remember the names of half the women I've been with. Usually, I leave their beds in the middle of the night, after we've had sex, so I won't have to remember. I leave them long before they can leave me."

"Wow."

"I always stay busy with my work, using that as an excuse for not ever committing to anyone, but that's not really it."

"What is it?"

"Women excite me. Then they quickly bore me. I have a high need for physical touch, for sex."

"In that way we're not alike."

"We're not?" she asked teasingly.

"I'm practically asexual. I've always envied people to whom touch came easily."

"And I've always envied people who weren't ruled by their sexual fantasies."

"Then we should make great friends."

We both laughed.

"Tell me about Gallagher. I want to know more about this

woman who was in your life," she requested, settling back into the booth.

"Well," I paused, trying to think about how I would begin, "we met four years ago playing on a softball team."

"Did you approach her or did she approach you — I love to know how women got together."

"Neither really. We started out as friends. Both of us needed a friend then. My lover Lisa had just moved to Los Angeles, and Gallagher had recently moved here from Boston."

"Were you physically attracted to her?"

"Oh God, yes! She's a beautiful woman!"

"What did you like best about her?"

"Physically, you mean?"

She nodded.

"Her shoulders, I guess. She has these great broad shoulders."

"What about your relationship — what was it like?"

"The first year was fantastic! I couldn't believe how happy I was. I kept expecting someone to come in and steal her away, but they never did. From practically our first date, Gallagher made it clear to me, and everyone else, that she was in love with me."

"Didn't that scare you, how much she cared about you?"

"It terrified me. It still does. None of my other relationships had prepared me for how much Gallagher loved me or for how loyal she was. She taught me a lot. About trust. And about passion."

"So you were passionate then?"

"Were we ever. I mean she's Italian, how could we not be? Our first year or so, we made love all the time. It was the happiest year of my life. I called it 'The Year of Passion.' "

"What happened?" I could see the concern on Destiny's face.

"The same thing that always happens, except this time, it was devastating for me, because I thought Gallagher was my life partner. Gradually I stopped being able to be close to her. We made love less and less and fought more and more."

"How sad."

"It *was* sad. Gallagher was in therapy trying to work through the effects her mother's physical abuse had on her. I was trying to sort out feelings about my family. Pretty soon, we were no longer in love, we were in therapy. It took over our lives."

"I know that feeling, like it's consuming your life."

"Exactly. How could two broken people keep all the pieces together? We couldn't. At first, our fights were funny, almost charming. Then, slowly, they became more desperate. One night, I found myself walking home in the rain because we'd had a fight and I refused to ride in the same car with her. I was fifteen miles from home, in a terrible neighborhood, at midnight. That's when I knew we'd gone too far. We were destroying each other."

"Was that why you ended the relationship?"

"Partially. Mostly, I ended it because too many things were broken. An alarm clock. A lamp. Our insides."

I fought back tears as I struggled to tell her the dark truth.

"One or both of us would go into these violent rages where we'd break things and push each other around. Finally, I couldn't take it anymore. I couldn't stand to be around the anger, in her or in me. We still brought out the good in each other, up until the day she left, but God, did we bring out the bad in each other, too."

"I've been in some pretty rough fights myself," she said, perhaps sensing my guilt.

"Not like ours you haven't. At least I hope you haven't."

"You'd be surprised." She reached out to calm my fingers which were drumming on the table. I recoiled inside, but I let her hand stay on mine.

"Thanks for saying that."

"I'm not just saying it to be kind, Kris. It's true."

"I always thought we were the only ones who took our anger that far."

"Not hardly."

Much to my relief, the waiter interrupted with our food, a vegetarian burrito for Destiny, chicken fajitas for me. After he left, I quickly changed the subject.

"Are you ready to hear a little about my time with your father and your grandma?"

"I guess so," Destiny answered, taking a deep breath.

"Okay. Stop me anytime it gets to be too much for you."

I started by summarizing my afternoon with her father. She interrupted me several times to ask questions.

"So they weren't able to have kids?"

"Right."

"But they never knew which of them was unable?"

"Right."

"Okay, go on."

And then later...

"So it really was my mother, more than my father, who

wanted to adopt me, is that right?"

"It seems so."

"That's strange."

"Why?"

"My father always seemed to enjoy me more. All these years, I assumed it was his idea to adopt. By nature, my mother's not a very warm person, but especially with me, it seemed like she kept her distance. I always felt like I wasn't good enough for her. When I was in high school, it finally dawned on me that she wasn't good enough for me either. Maybe because she wasn't my real mother, mostly because she was the kind of mother she was. Now, I can ignore her every time she tells me I should do something different with my life, but it took me twenty years to get to the point where I didn't jump every time she said that."

"Funny, isn't it, how when we're kids, we think we failed our parents, but as adults, we realize they failed us," I interjected.

"That is funny. It's even worse when you're adopted, though, because you have the added paranoia of thinking they don't love you as much because you aren't their natural child. And every time they disappoint you, you fantasize about what your 'real' parents would have been like. I never quite got past feeling like a guest in the Greaves' home. My parents, especially my father, tried to make me welcome, but I never completely felt like I was. I spent a lot of my childhood escaping into fantasies. I've never told anyone this, but all of my friends, my true friends, were imaginary people. They were people I made up in my head, friends who never left me. It's ironic really," she laughed bitterly, "my only permanent relationships have been with people who don't even exist."

I think if she could have cried then, she would have. I must have been reading her mind.

"Damn it all!" She hit the table with her open hand. "I wish I could cry, but I can't. I never have been able to. Sometimes, so much emotion backs up in me I think I'll explode!"

"You cried when you were little. Maybe you'll learn to cry again."

"Did I really?"

"Yes, you did. Your grandmother told me you cried after your parents died."

"Huh. I wonder why I stopped."

"I don't know."

"I never cry. Sometimes I'll feel like it, like just now, but the tears won't come. They simply will not come out of me," she said angrily.

We were both quiet for a moment. Her voice broke the silence.

"Hey, Kris, if you could change just one thing about yourself, what would it be?"

"Seriously?"

"Yes, seriously, what would you change?"

I thought before I answered. "I'd touch more," I said, my voice cracking, much to my embarrassment.

"I'd cry more," Destiny said and looked away. "That's what I was thinking about a minute ago."

There was more silence, as if we'd both said too much.

"But enough about me," she exclaimed, the false enthusiasm apparent. "Tell me about my grandmother. What's she like?"

"She's quite spirited actually. I see where you get your drive. She's one tough lady."

I went on to tell her all about Marie Kenwood. I left out the details of their good-bye scene, because frankly, I thought it was more than Destiny could take. She laughed when I told her about my great detective work in figuring out I was sitting in her grandma's favorite spot. She had a million questions for me. I could barely answer one before she fired off another.

"Where does she live?"

"In a townhouse in southeast Denver, near Iliff and —"

"What's the townhouse look like?"

"It's brick, two-story —"

"No, no. Inside, what's it look like inside?"

"Basically like you'd expect an older woman's home to look like. Wingback chairs, coffee table full of ladies magazines —"

"What's she look like?"

"She's short but imposing. She's quite attractive, very dignified looking. Her nails are manicured —"

"Do I look like her?"

"Not really, Destiny." I saw the disappointment in her eyes. "She's over eighty years old. She has more wrinkles than you." I tried to cheer her up, but the disappointment remained. "Maybe you look like her a little."

She visibly brightened.

"What part of me?"

I said the first thing that came to my mind.

"Your eyes. They look like hers. Not much, but a little."

She smiled widely.

58

"We were close then, she and I?"

"Very close," I said without having to lie.

"I wish I could remember her," Destiny said with a faraway, dreamy look in her eyes.

"You don't remember anything about your grandma?"

"No, not at all. It's like she belongs to someone else."

"In a sense, she does. The little girl who knew your grandma doesn't exist right now, because you buried her with your parents."

"I guess I did," she said quietly. "My first conscious memory is of kindergarten, my first day of school. I was Destiny Greaves by then. Peter and Barbara Kenwood were gone. Destiny Kenwood was gone, too."

"You know, Destiny, there's no way to minimize how much tragedy there's been in your life, but there is a bright spot: You were loved. It's clear your parents loved each other and they loved you. Your grandma adored you, too. That's something, you know."

"If she loved me so much, why did she let me go?"

"I don't think she had much choice. She was a widow who had lost both her husband and her son in less than a year. Plus, she didn't know she'd never see you again. It wasn't until after they took you away that the Sisters told her she should never contact you. That it was in your best interest —"

"In my best interest!" she practically shouted. "What did anyone know about my best interest?"

"Not much, it seems." This time, I reached across the table to take her hand.

"She could have fought for me," the little one protested, pulling her hand away.

"No, she couldn't, Destiny, or she would have. She loved you, she wanted you, but she didn't know what else to do except bundle you up and give you to the Sisters."

"When you saw her...." she hesitated before finishing the question.

"Yes...." I gently prodded her.

"When you saw her... did she ask about me?"

In that one question, I saw all the vulnerability of the young child in her.

"No, she didn't," I answered, wincing at the hurt look she gave me. "I think she wanted to, but she couldn't bring herself to do it. But if you'd like to meet her, I could try to set something up."

59

"No," she said softly. "Let's get out of here."

With that, we left, having barely touched our food.

All the way home from Nadine's, I thought about parenting.

Despite my memory loss, I knew my mother had been a terrible parent. I could remember her locking us out of the house for hours on end. In the winter, we'd sit by the dryer vent for warmth. I could remember her kidding with people about what a rotten child I was and how she wanted to be rid of me. Except she wasn't kidding.

It took becoming an adult for me to realize that I hated my mom most of all for not loving me.

I tried to sort out my feelings about my father, but they were more confusing. He hadn't been a perfect father, but he had loved me. This much, I knew. I vividly remembered all the times he rubbed my back or had me scratch his head. I knew he'd been loving, but that's as far as I could bear to look into the past with him.

What if he, too, had hurt me? What then?

When I got home, I went straight to bed, but I didn't sleep well.

Driving in the car with Mom and Dad. I'm asking Dad why my brother David and my sister Jill work for him. I'm asking him why he is paying them a sales bonus if my older sisters Ann and Gail and I are the salespeople.

In his familiar way, he ignores me, saying he doesn't see any connection. It's none of my business. It is my business, though, I argue, because I own the company. I want fairness. I want things to be explainable.

My dad becomes so riled by my questions that he turns around and spits this huge amount of liquid into the air. I'm in the back seat. He's driving. The liquid rains down over me. My mom is shocked but doesn't really say or do anything. I'm stunned and completely humiliated. I immediately hop out of the car and start walking back.

It's a long walk down some dirt road in the mountains. I'm sobbing and sobbing. I'm happy that I'm wearing a hooded jacket. The grotesque liquid doesn't touch me much. Just on the outside. I'm careful how I move so it won't touch my flesh.

CHAPTER

8

When I came into work the next morning, there was a message waiting for me that Destiny had called. Before I started working, I rang her back.

"Kris, you'll never believe this — I had the most incredible dream last night. I dreamed about my grandma. I saw her for the first time. I saw how beautiful she is. We were together, laughing and playing in this big, old house. It's like I was a little girl, except I was my age now. I had to leave her to go to this convention I'm going to next month. It was really cold outside. I didn't want to go, but I knew leaving was the best thing for me. She was crying and I was crying. Can you believe that? I was actually crying, even if it was only in a dream."

Before I could answer, she continued.

"My grandma told me not to cry. She told me my new family wouldn't want to see me cry, which made no sense in my dream, because I was only going to a silly convention. But then, she hugged me tight and I felt so safe. I knew I'd be all right. It was a wonderful dream. It felt good to cry. What do you think of it?"

"Oh, my God," was all I could say.

"What, Kris, what is it?"

"That's it!"

"That's what?"

"That's why you can't cry."

"*What's* why I can't cry?"

"Your grandma told you not to cry."

"I know, Kris, but it was only a dream."

"No, no, not in the dream. In real life. I didn't tell you this last night, because I didn't think you were ready for it, but obviously you are. You've started to process it."

"Process *what*?"

"She told you not to cry. That's why you stopped crying. The day the nuns came to get you was the coldest day of winter, according to your grandma. When you started to cry, your grandma told you that your new family wouldn't want to see you cry. You took that literally and never cried in front of the Greaves. Your dad said you used to cry at night but as soon as someone came into the room, you stopped. That's it! I never made the connection before, but that's it!"

"Oh, no!" were the only words I heard for a long time, repeated over and over again.

"You obeyed her too well."

No response.

"Destiny, are you there?"

Still no response.

"Destiny!" I was starting to get alarmed.

"I think I'm crying, Kris. Not a lot, but a little," she said faintly.

"That's great!" I shouted. "You're crying! That's wonderful!"

"I had a memory. Thanks to you, I had a memory. I can't believe I had a memory, even if it was in my dreams," she sounded excited. "Now I'm laughing and crying at the same time. What the hell's the matter with me?"

"Nothing is. Not one thing. You're going to be fine."

"You think a memory counts if it's in a dream?"

"Of course it does. A memory is a memory, no matter what form it comes in," I said, and instantly felt sick to my stomach with the realization of what I'd just said.

"Isn't it funny that part of what I dreamed was about my life today, and the other part was about the past?"

I wasn't listening anymore. I could hardly breathe. As fast as I could, I said good-bye, got off the phone and ran to the bathroom. I closed the door and threw up.

• • •

As I was coming out of the bathroom, I ran into Ann.
She looked at me with concern.

62

"Are you okay, Kris?"

"I just threw up."

"Are you sick?"

"I wouldn't have thrown up if I wasn't sick."

"No, I meant do you have the flu or something."

"I don't think so."

"Maybe it was something you ate."

"Maybe," I said vaguely and excused myself, trying to get back to the solace of my private office.

As I was walking down the hall, her voice stopped me.

"Hey, Kris...."

"Yes, Ann?" I waited with exaggerated patience.

"You're starting to look a little run down lately. Are you sure you're okay?"

"I'm fine," I lied.

"Is it that case you're working on? Is it Destiny?"

"I wish it were that simple," I said, the fatigue evident in the slowness of my words. "Really, Ann, I'm fine. When I can, I'll tell you all about it."

She knew enough not to push me any further.

"Remember, you can talk to me if you need to, Kris."

I wanted to believe her, but I couldn't.

She saw the disbelief in my eyes. I turned and continued walking down the long, narrow hallway.

When we were kids, Ann and I had never been close. She and Gail had shared a room and a life. I was no part of either. They were good friends and I was the outsider.

It wasn't until after we'd both moved out of the house we grew up in, that slowly but surely, Ann and I had managed to forge a friendship, based mostly on working together. Still, I never completely trusted her. After all, she, too, had come from the same abusive environment.

• • •

I spent the afternoon in my office with the door and the blinds closed. Ostensibly, I was working on a marketing piece. In fact, I wasn't doing much of anything. I was doodling on a legal pad and sipping soda to settle my stomach when Michelle called to remind me that we were meeting that night for dinner. It was a good thing she called — I'd completely forgotten that we had plans.

63

I wasn't in the mood to go out to dinner with her, particularly since I knew I'd have to listen to her psychic's predictions, but I'd promised, so off I went at the appointed hour.

"You look tired," Michelle greeted me as I ambled into Gaylords Grille, our favorite restaurant.

"You look radiant!" I said and she did.

I tried to think what was different about her, but I couldn't pinpoint it. Her outfit was the same as always: loose-fitting rust colored mock-sweats, forest green turtleneck, and a large-print, floral pattern light jacket. Several years back, she'd had her colors done and since then had refused to wear any color other than fall colors: rust, green, gold, brown. She'd even convinced me that I should wear brighter colors and most of the time, I followed her advice. That night, I was wearing a purple long-sleeved sports shirt, a fluorescent pink and teal pull-over coat, and my usual faded blue jeans and Topsiders.

Maybe it was her hair; it looked good that night, which wasn't always the case. In her driver's license picture, the truth was recorded: Michelle Spivack had bone-straight hair. But because Michelle hated straight hair ("It makes my nose look even bigger than it is"), she was constantly trying new variations of perms. Her current one was tight and curly and she was wearing her dark brown hair at shoulder length. Behind the curls, I could see the diamond posts she always wore. I noticed she was wearing her contacts, not her usual wire-rimmed, round frame eyeglasses. Whenever Michelle fell in love, her worst vanity showed through.

"Love, or lust, must be agreeing with you," I added.

A shadow crossed Michelle's face but she smiled brightly.

"It is! Destiny's wonderful," she said as the waitress showed us to our table.

Once seated, it took us about two seconds to decide what to eat. We both ordered our usual: black bean dip and tortilla chips to start, Monte Cristo and ice tea for Michelle, Caesar salad and Virgin Mary for me. It was nice to have routines.

"I can't wait for the three of us to get together," Michelle said after the waitress was out of earshot.

"Not until the case is over," I warned.

"Not until then," Michelle agreed. "But hopefully, that should be soon."

"Oh?" News to me and I was supposed to be in charge.

"I went to the psychic, remember?"

"I remember," I said impatiently.

"She had a lot of good feedback."

"Oh, sure!"

"Do you want to hear this or not, Kris?" Michelle looked pained.

"I'm sorry." I gave her my most charming smile. "What did Joanne have to say?"

"Zelda, she calls herself Zelda now."

"All right!" Now I was pained. "What did Zelda have to say?"

"Well, first I asked about Destiny's father," Michelle said eagerly, leaning over the table.

I moved my ice water out of the reach of her enthusiasm. "And?"

"And she couldn't get a reading on him. It was extraordinary. There was absolutely no reading on him. No father figure in Destiny's life. No biological father anyway."

"That's strange." Despite myself, I was hooked on this crackpot's tips. According to Marie Kenwood, Destiny and her father were quite close. But of course, I reminded myself, this was a mother's opinion of her dead son. Perhaps I'd return and question her more closely.

"Isn't it? And her mother — this is the best part — she and Destiny are very close, even today. They always have been, except for some period that Zelda couldn't see very clearly. Since Destiny's mother is dead, she thinks Destiny and her mother must be spiritually connected. Isn't that exciting?" Michelle bubbled.

"Very exciting," I said with absolutely no sarcasm in my voice. Then, my true feelings came out, "Did you pay good money for this vision?"

"Of course I did," Michelle retorted. "She *is* a professional, you know. She advertises all over the community. She even has business cards."

"Business cards cost fifteen bucks, Michelle," I felt compelled to point out.

"Still, it shows a commitment to her work."

"True," I gave in, not because I believed fifteen dollars was a serious commitment, but because I knew I couldn't win this argument. "What did the big Z have to say about you and Destiny? What's in your future?"

Michelle grimaced. "She said 'Enjoy Destiny. She is a gift.' "

"That's all? What's that supposed to mean?"

"She wouldn't tell me anything more. You don't suppose it means we're going to break up, do you, Kris?"

I could no longer conceal my total exasperation.

"How am I supposed to know? I'm not psychic."

"I hope that's not what she meant. I'm crazy about Destiny. I'm not sure if she's crazy about me. I mean I know she likes me, but I don't know how much?"

"What's Destiny think about what the psychic said?"

"The part about us or about her family?"

"Both."

"She laughed at the part about us. She said she'd never thought of herself before as a gift."

"What about her family?"

"She said that was interesting, but it didn't seem to impress her," Michelle said, sounding a little offended.

"It *is* a bit vague, Michelle," I defended Destiny's skepticism because it mirrored my own.

At that moment, I had no way of knowing how prophetic the information would turn out to be.

"Not to a believer. A believer would understand its value," she said adamantly, pointing her finger.

"Maybe," I shrugged my shoulders.

That pretty much ended our talk about the psychic. We were at an impasse as we'd been so many times in the past, both of us stubbornly believing our belief was the only one.

We moved on to safer subjects. Her work: She'd just been ranked the top salesperson in her medical equipment company. My work: I'd just hired another graphic artist. Gallagher: No, I hadn't heard from her and I had no plans to call her.

We ended the meal with our usual desert: one piece of black bottom pie, two forks.

• • •

Over the weekend, I did nothing except ride my bike and sleep a lot. I didn't work on Destiny's case. I needed a rest from it. She never called me. Maybe she needed a break from it, too.

On Monday, as I was reviewing logos for a chiropractor, Ann knocked on my door.

"Kris, there's a Marie Kenwood for you on line one."

Startled, I pushed my work aside and answered the phone.

66

"Hello, Mrs. Kenwood, this is Kristin," I said cheerfully.

"Of course it's you, young lady, you're the one I asked for."

How was it that this woman I barely knew always managed, in ten seconds or less, to make me feel like a little kid?

"Can I help you with something?" I asked, trying to sound as adult-like as possible.

"Yes, you may. I want to see Destiny," she barked.

I should have expected it, I guess, but still, her request took me by surprise.

"You want to meet Destiny?"

"I've already met her. Now, I want to see her. Can you set up a time for us to get together?"

"Why me?"

"Because I don't have her phone number —"

"I could give it to you," I quickly interjected, thinking I'd have to get Destiny's permission first.

"— and because I don't want to shock the poor girl as much as I'm obviously shocking you."

"This is a shock. It's been a lot of years. Why didn't you ask me the other day?"

"When you get to be my age, you don't do many things impetuously. I wanted to think about it before I asked. Now I've thought about it and I want to see her."

"Why haven't you contacted her before now?"

"I didn't want to upset her or myself. I've seen her on the news, but it seemed better to let the past be the past."

"Why now then?" I repeated.

"Because I miss the little one," she said, sadness replacing the brusqueness in her voice. "When Destiny was taken from me, I put her out of my mind and went on with my life. The pain never went away, but in time I was able to stop thinking about her and Peter. Then, all this time later, you come into my life asking questions. You reminded me that I care about her — not the Destiny Greaves on the news, the Destiny Kenwood I used to hold in my arms. That's the Destiny I know. I want to see the Destiny I don't know. Do you think you can arrange it or not?"

I hesitated before answering her.

"I'll try."

"I'm not getting any younger, young lady."

"I know that, Mrs. Kenwood," I chuckled. "I'll talk to Destiny."

"She trusts you, doesn't she?"

"I hope so."

"I'd like to have her over for dinner some night this week. What night do you think would be good?"

"I don't know, Mrs. Kenwood. I really don't. I'll talk to Destiny. That's all I can do. The instant I know Destiny's answer, you'll know."

"Thank you."

"Don't thank me yet. I haven't done anything."

"Don't be so modest. Of course you have, Kristin," she said, using my name for the first time. "Destiny's lucky to have a friend like you. By the way, you can come to dinner, too, if you'd like. Tomorrow night would be best for me."

With that, she hung up.

•••

Immediately, I called Destiny at work. As I waited on hold while Destiny's assistant checked to see if she was in, I marvelled at Mrs. Kenwood's request. The dinner invitation had really been more of an order. I wondered if people were born with that kind of gall, or if it came with age. As I was pondering this, the assistant came back on the line and told me Destiny was out of the office. I left a message, asked her to mark it "urgent," and then tried to get some work done. Every time the phone rang, I hoped it would be her.

I was gathering my things and getting ready to go home early when, much to my surprise, Destiny appeared in the flesh.

"Hi, Kris. I hope I'm not bothering you stopping in like this."

"Not at all. I left a message for you earlier."

"I know, I called in and got my messages. I had to come out this way anyway, so I thought I'd come see you in person."

"Great! Come on in, we can talk in my office."

"I'm sorry, I can't stay. I've just got a second. I've got to be to the Capitol in fifteen minutes. What's up?"

"You're never going to believe this!"

"What?"

"Your grandma wants to see you!" I presented the words to her like a gift, thinking she'd cross the room and joyfully hug me.

She didn't. She leaned against the door and quietly asked, "She does?" In those two words, I could hear confusion, nervousness, and fear.

"She called me this morning. She asked me to set up a time for the two of you to get together. You'll go, won't you?"

68

"You didn't call her, Kris? You didn't set this whole thing up?"

"No, of course not. I wouldn't go that far."

"Why does she want to see me?" Destiny asked, her voice full of suspicion.

"You're her only granddaughter."

"I always have been," she said curtly, sounding like her older relative. "Why now?"

"I asked her the same thing — she wants to see you now because she misses you. Until I came into her life last week, she didn't remember how much she cares. Now she does."

"Huh," she grunted, folding her arms across her chest.

"Will you see her?"

"I don't know. I'm not sure I'm ready."

"She's not getting any younger, you know," I found myself parroting her grandmother's words.

"I take it you think I should do this." There was an edge to her voice, one that bordered on coldness.

"Is it that obvious?"

"No kidding!"

"I'm sorry. Maybe I'm carried away by the excitement of it all. I have this fantasy that you and your grandma will meet after all these years, hug each other, and live happily ever after, eternally grateful to me for bringing you together."

"It isn't that easy."

"I know," I said quietly, trying to hide my disappointment.

"Do you think she'll like me?"

"Oh, God, yes! What's not to like? You're a remarkable woman. She'll love you!"

"I'm also a lesbian."

"Destiny, you're the most famous lesbian in Denver. Your name's always in the news. She must know you're a lesbian. She told me she's followed your career. How could she not know?"

"I guess you're right."

"Of course I'm right, but if you want, I'll call her and ask her if she wants to see you even though you're a lesbian."

"It is kind of absurd, isn't it, that this is what I worry about?" She gave me a half smile.

"It could be worse. You could be worrying that she's a lesbian, too."

We both laughed.

"What if I do see her, Kris? What next? Do I have to go to her house every Sunday for dinner? Do I have to drive her to church?

Do I have to care for her when she gets sick?"

"Whoa, whoa!" I put up a hand to slow down her thoughts.

"I can't take all that. I really can't. That's too much commitment for me." The words spilled out of her.

"Destiny, slow down. You're way ahead of yourself here with worry. I'll set up a dinner, one dinner, that's all. You can just see how that goes first."

"One dinner?" she asked meekly.

"One dinner. I promise that's it. We'll take this one small, safe step at a time. We'll go as far as you can go, then we'll see if you can go any further."

"Okay."

"That means you'll do it?" I asked, letting the excitement creep back into my voice.

"I'll do it...."

"Great!" I started to cross the room to hug her.

"Not so fast, Kris. I'll do it on one condition...."

Not so great. I stopped dead in my tracks.

"What is it?" I asked and this time, my arms were folded.

"You have to come with me."

"Me?" My voice cracked.

"Yes, you. Will you come with me?"

"But don't you want to be alone with her the first time you meet?" I asked, using my most persuasive sales voice.

"No, I don't. I'm scared to death to meet her. I need you to come with me. Can you do it or not?"

"Of course I can. How does tomorrow night sound?" The words were out of my mouth before I had a chance to consider them.

"That would work. Thanks for everything, Kris. You're a good woman. Now I've got to run. Call me when you've set a time, and do it soon before I change my mind."

"I hear you," I said.

I called Marie Kenwood back and told her Destiny and I would join her for dinner. I tried to talk her in to letting us take her out to eat, but she wouldn't hear of it. She insisted we come to her house for a home-cooked meal.

Briefly, I wondered if I was getting too involved in this case, but as soon as the thought entered my mind, I dismissed it.

CHAPTER

9

Because I knew my way to Marie Kenwood's, I drove and picked up Destiny on the way.

She lived just a few miles from me in a great old mansion in Capitol Hill. Built in 1896 for one very wealthy family, the place was now home to Destiny and four other women, each of whom had a separate residence. With her parents' help, Destiny had bought the house a year earlier, when Denver's real estate prices were at their lowest. One of the women who lived there was a carpenter, so she renovated in exchange for rent. One room at a time, she was restoring the building to its original majesty. Destiny told me all of this as she gave me a tour.

She lived in what was once the living room, dining room, and receiving room (for receiving guests, not packages). In the old living room, she had a fifteen foot long fireplace, and an entire wall of windows. She slept in the former dining room, using the built in china hutch as a dresser. The ceilings in every room were twelve feet tall.

There was clutter everywhere, but the place wasn't messy. Just full. She had tons of furniture, none of which matched ("I have a weakness for garage sales and Capitol Hill has the best garage sales in the world"). But her place was comfortable and, for a second, I wished I lived there instead of in my high-rise, high-tech environment.

In the car, we didn't talk much. I tried to initiate conversation on a variety of topics: the front page news, her work, my work, but none of it seemed to interest her. When we were close to her grandma's house, I gave up on the mundane and got right to the heart of it.

"Are you nervous, Destiny?"

"A little. Do you think I'm doing the right thing?"

I nodded, though I wasn't sure.

"All day I've been thinking about this dinner," she said, never looking at me, her eyes riveted on the road ahead. "I've been wondering if what I'm doing is the right thing, if I should ever have hired you."

I didn't say anything. I had my own ambivalent thoughts about the merits of crawling back into the past.

"It's easy to wish I hadn't ever started asking the questions. It's easy to live my life as I've always lived it. What's much harder is this change, these confrontations. Without them, my life would go on as usual — with holes in it, but without this risk. One day, I woke up and decided the holes were too big. That's the day I called you, Kris.

"But so many days since then, I've woken up, slapped myself on the forehead and said 'What the hell were you thinking, Destiny? What are you doing to yourself?' Because this, what I'm doing here, this is the hardest thing I've ever done. So hard that most days, the holes don't seem so big after all, and I want to stop. Does any of this make sense?"

I nodded, afraid to say that it made all the sense in the world to me, that every day I asked myself the same question. I'd thought my life was empty, so I'd started looking into my past, hoping to find the source of the emptiness. Yet, the more I looked, the more sources I found, and the larger the emptiness seemed. The holes I'd sought to fill, instead seemed to grow bigger, big enough to consume me, I sometimes feared.

I knew all too well what Destiny Greaves was afraid of, but I couldn't say that to her. Not then. Not as we were pulling into her grandmother's driveway.

"I'll be right here with you," I reached over to squeeze her hand. "You say the word and we're outta here, okay?"

"Okay." She gave me a weak smile.

Before we could make it to Marie Kenwood's porch, the door flew open.

"You're early," the older woman said. She looked at her watch. "Three minutes to be exact."

What was it with this time fixation? Maybe it was her way of

72

covering her nervousness, I thought forgivingly.

"We would have been here later," I said lightly, "but I knew my way this time."

My humor was in vain. No one was listening to me. She and Destiny just stood looking at each other. I couldn't read the emotion in either of their faces. I broke the silence with formal introductions.

"Mrs. Kenwood, this is Destiny Greaves —" I began.

"Of course it is," she snapped. "Who else would it be? You look just the same."

"Do I really?" Destiny asked timidly.

"In the face you do. Come in out of the cold, both of you."

With that, without touching Destiny, she ushered us into the living room, took our coats, and carried them off into another room. I stole a quick look at Destiny, pointed to Marie's favorite spot on the couch, and raised one eyebrow. She understood perfectly. As she sat down in a burgundy wingback chair, she struggled to conceal her laughter. I sat next to her in the wingback's twin.

We'd barely made ourselves comfortable when Mrs. Kenwood came back into the room and ordered us into the dining room. There, we ate a pleasant dinner of ham and scalloped potatoes and managed to keep the conversation going with a minimum dose of awkwardness. I say "we" but it was mostly the two Kenwoods. Neither of them paid much attention to me and I accommodated their need to talk by limiting myself to innocuous smiles and head noddings. Destiny winked at me a few times to let me know she was glad I had come, but otherwise she was absorbed with knowing all there was to know about her grandmother.

They talked all about Destiny's work for the community, Mrs. Kenwood often interrupting with "You always were like that, Destiny."

After we'd eaten, Marie Kenwood impressed me and embarrassed Destiny when she pulled out an album of newspaper clippings, all articles relating to Destiny's accomplishments. The achievements began when Destiny was arrested for going shirtless in Cheeseman Park (she was part of a demonstration for equal rights for women) and ended with an award she'd been given a month earlier for her successes in furthering the rights of lesbian women.

At one point, Mrs. Kenwood delicately asked Destiny if there was anyone special in her life. Destiny looked squarely at me and smiled faintly before she answered, "No, I'm afraid not, but I have a giant crush on someone. I just haven't had the courage to tell her yet."

"Well, you should, honey. I'm sure she'd like you back."

"Maybe," Destiny replied and again stared at me, almost tauntingly, her gaze unflinching.

My God, I thought, I think she means me. But how could she? She was dating Michelle, my friend of ten years. Maybe she was the one Destiny was talking about. But if that was the case, why wouldn't she tell the woman she was sleeping with that she had a crush on her. No, it couldn't be Michelle. But God, don't let it be me. All of this raced through my mind at lightening speed.

To slow down the beating of my heart, I excused myself and went to the bathroom. Once there, I put the toilet seat down and sat on it, fully clothed. I leaned over and put my head between my knees, struggling to regain my breath.

"Calm down, Kris, I'm sure you're reading too much into this," I repeated to myself. When I was somewhat under control, I flushed the toilet for effect, checked my appearance in the rose-lined mirror, and rejoined Destiny and her grandmother.

I returned in time to see coffee being served in the living room.

Just as Destiny and I seated ourselves, Marie Kenwood excused herself.

"You were in the bathroom a long time, Kris. Are you okay?" Destiny asked me, almost teasingly, as if she knew exactly what had sent me running.

"I'm fine," I said, then quickly changed the subject. "What do you think of your grandma?" I asked in a low voice.

"I like her," Destiny whispered. "She's quite a woman."

"Now you know where you get it from."

She smiled.

"Does she seem familiar to you?" I leaned across the end table to ask her.

Destiny drew alarmingly close to me.

"Not in the least, but I'm having fun."

We giggled.

"Are you sure this is the right grandmother?" she asked behind a cupped hand, her lips almost touching my ear.

We giggled some more.

"It is. Or at least, it's the only one I could find on short notice."
With that, we laughed some more. For those precious few

seconds, we were like schoolgirls. Everything we said seemed hilarious to us, perhaps because reality itself was so unreal.

"I feel like I'm in the Twilight Zone, like I'm peeking in on someone else's life," Destiny said seriously.

Under my breath, I started humming the theme to the Twilight Zone, and we cracked up again.

Just then, Destiny's grandmother walked into the room carrying a large box. She motioned to us to join her on the couch and we did. Destiny sat next to her; I sat next to Destiny.

Mrs. Kenwood began to empty out the contents of the container. Non-stop, she talked as she showed us each item.

"Here's Mousie," she said showing us a stuffed mouse with one eye and one ear half chewed off. "Mousie went everywhere with you. This was my grandmother's wedding ring. I'd like you to have it." She carefully slipped the thin gold band on Destiny's little finger.

"These are pictures taken on your mom and dad's wedding day. Weren't they a happy couple? Here's your baby book. Your mother wrote in it faithfully. I saved all of this for you. All these years, Destiny, I knew I'd see you again."

It was clear Marie Kenwood was in another world, a world neither I nor Destiny understood well enough to visit with her.

When I first saw the box of memories, I'd gotten butterflies in my stomach. "This is it," I thought. "This is what will trigger Destiny's memory." But it didn't.

As if she were detached from the life the mementos represented, Destiny playfully examined the merchandise. She held Mousie in her arms. She twisted the ring on her finger. She oohed and aahed at the pictures of her parents. She leafed through the baby book. And none of it had any emotional effect on her. Not one piece of it. The memories were hidden too deep to be touched, even by physical pieces of her childhood.

When I saw that she couldn't be touched, I was at once disappointed and relieved.

Soon it was time for us to go. We repacked the box and I carried it to the car and then came back to get Destiny. We thanked Mrs. Kenwood for an enjoyable evening. Not quite sure what to say next, we three were silent until Destiny's strong voice cut through the night's quiet.

"I really enjoyed myself tonight. I'm sorry we didn't see each other sooner."

Marie Kenwood reached out to embrace Destiny.

"I've missed you, little one," she said quietly.

"Me, too, Nana," Destiny answered and then pulled back abruptly. "Where did that come from? Where did that name come from, Kris?" she asked, looking slightly hysterical.

"You remembered it, Destiny." And she had. I'd never mentioned the name in my talks with her.

"Oh, no," was all she could say as she trembled for a moment and then ran to the car.

Marie Kenwood just stood there stunned, her arms still outstretched, holding nothing. Then, her hands slowly fell to her side, almost like she'd given up. She softly said goodnight to me and then went inside the house.

After I got in the car and started the engine, Destiny instructed me to drive as fast as I could. Without delay, I got us out of there. I drove her home as quickly as was legal, the whole way torn between watching the road and watching her shake beside me.

CHAPTER

10

"That must have been hard on you," I said when we got back to her house.

We were comfortably seated on one of her sofas. She'd started a fire — three logs which looked like toothpicks in her massive fireplace — and served us drinks. Tea for her, Dr. Pepper for me.

"No problem." She grimaced. "Actually, it was the hardest thing I've ever done."

"That's saying a lot. You've done some pretty hard things."

"None that compare to this."

"For a minute there, I thought you were going to start crying."

"Who me? Never!"

I looked at her, my eyebrows raised.

"For a second, I did feel like crying, but I couldn't. Not in front of her. Not when I didn't know her."

"She is your grandmother, Destiny. Maybe you could have comforted each other."

"I don't think we could have. It's too late for that."

"Maybe so," I agreed reluctantly.

"Can I ask you something, Kris?"

"It's not about Gallagher, is it?" I asked, my guard up.

"No," she laughed. "Not this time."

"Okay, then."

"What made you decide to take this case? Why did you want to help me?"

I didn't answer right away. When I did, I started with the

easy, obvious reasons, hoping to avoid the harder ones.

"Well... you were a friend of Michelle's...."

Long pause.

"... and I've always admired you from afar."

That made her laugh.

"No, really," I protested. "The work you're doing is important."

"Is that all?" Her eyes seemed to bore a hole through my thoughts.

"Er, no," I fumbled for the right words. "I wanted to give you back your childhood, Destiny... and I'm not sure if I should say this...."

"Go on," her gentle voice pushed me.

"I wanted to get back my own, too." I let go of her steady gaze.

"What do you mean?"

"I don't have any memory either — not of the first seven years of my life, anyway." I was starting to sweat.

"Why not?" She reached out to calm my fidgeting hands.

"I don't know."

"Did something traumatic happen to you when you were little, Kris?"

"Yes! No! I don't know!"

"What happened?"

"Nothing happened! Everything happened!" I screamed, startled at the anger in my own voice.

The exhaustion of the past month was starting to catch up to me. I was on the edge and I knew it.

"When you started helping me, the memories started coming back for you, too, didn't they?" Her words were as soft as her touch.

"How did you know?" My voice quivered.

"Every time I see you, you look like I feel: more tired and more scared. Are you sleeping at night?"

"Not much."

"What's scaring you?"

I shook my head violently.

"Whatever it is, it can't be that bad."

"Oh, it is." I nodded my head vehemently. "Every night, I close my eyes, but I never sleep for long. The images... they're awful. How could such horrible things happen at night after a little girl closes her eyes?"

"What things?"

"Oh, no, I can't say." In a monotone, I started to chant, "No way, can't say, no way, can't say —"

"Kris, please, let me in just a little. I trusted you — trust me!"

"No way, can't say, no way, can't say —"

"Try!" she implored. "Try!"

I stopped my chant, but for the longest time, I couldn't say anything. I just clutched the loose jean material near my right thigh, then let it go, clutched it and let it go. Finally, there was the crystal clear sound of a voice, a voice that cracked and shook as it learned to speak.

"I think I was abused when I was young."

She didn't say anything.

"Sexually abused," I added.

Still, she was silent. Perhaps she knew that if I stopped speaking, I'd never start again.

"By my father." There. After a lifetime of silence, the words were out. Life-changing words that could never be taken back.

I breathed for the first time.

"I'm so sorry, Kris. I'm so sorry for you." Destiny began to cry.

"I can't sleep anymore because every time I close my eyes, I'm afraid someone will attack me and he does, in my dreams. I'm so tired, so utterly, completely exhausted from the terror. All I want, more than anything else in this world, is to have a safe place to sleep. I want my own bed, in my own room, to be a safe place, but it's not."

Destiny shivered but didn't say anything.

"I've never slept well, but I've never had night terrors like these. I hate the darkness. Most nights, I'm awake half the night. I try to think about work. It's the only thing that makes me happy. I plot how much money I'll make and try to forget about what woke me up. The next day, I can barely work. I go home early to nap. It's only safe for me to sleep when it's light outside and I'm on my couch in the living room."

"I'm so sorry, Kris. I'm sorry if I brought this on," she said between tears. My own eyes were as dry as the crackling fire.

"You didn't," I snapped. "He did. My father did. When I took your case, I was scared to death something like this might happen and it has, but I had to do something."

"Does Michelle know?"

"No. No one knows. I don't have proof, just flashes of memories I can't accept. For a long time, on some level, I guess I've suspected something happened because of what I can remember, how my father used to walk around in his underwear, how he wasn't affectionate with my mom, but was overly affectionate with us kids, things like that. But I've never had a conscious memory of the abuse. I blocked it too well. Only at night do I get my clues, in my dreams. I know it's him in my dreams. It has to be him.

"Don't you see, Destiny, my memory loss is the most incriminating evidence of all against my father. I've blocked the horror from my mind, and everything else, too. Last year, my grandma told me about the first time my brother David had an epileptic seizure. He was three then and I was six. We were all in a restaurant and he slid off the booth, writhing and convulsing. At the time, they had no idea it was epilepsy. They thought he was dying. They called an ambulance and rushed him to the hospital. I was there the whole time, and I can't remember one bit of it. Neither can my sister Ann, and my God, she was eight years old. Whatever he did to me, he must have stopped when I was seven, because that's when my memory starts."

"What do you think made him stop?"

"I don't know. Maybe my mother caught him — that's right around the time she started spending so much time in bed. It's all so vague. Unfortunately, my only clues come from these horrible dreams."

"Is there anyone you can talk to when you have these dreams?"

Wearily, I shook my head.

"I can't. Who's awake at 3 a.m.?"

"I am."

"You are not!"

"I'm an insomniac."

"Michelle told me you sleep like a log."

"Okay, so I lied. I'm not usually awake in the middle of the night, but I could be. You could call me."

"I couldn't, Destiny. I just couldn't. What if...." I couldn't bring myself to finish the sentence.

"What if what?"

"What if my dream's graphic? Wouldn't that make you sick?"

"Not at all."

"And you're not just trying to even things up? I helped you and now you'll help me?" I asked, regretting the question even as it left my mouth.

"This may be foreign to you, Kris, but I'm trying to be your friend," she said with a trace of anger.

80

"I'm sorry, Destiny." I started to cry.

She came closer to me and held me, tentatively at first, then more tightly.

The tighter she held me, the more I cried.

"Please call me. If it happens again, promise you'll call me."

"I will," I said. "Or at least I'll try."

"I called you about my dream. You were the first one to hear me cry. A historic moment. You owe me, Kristin Ashe," she joked.

"I'll call," I said, not really sure I would.

●●●

All the way home, I thought about what it meant to be a "victim of incest." I hated both those words. Victim. Incest. I hated people who saw themselves as victims. I would not be one of them. I hated the thought of incest. How could it have happened to me? Over and over again, I tried on the words for size, hoping they would fit, praying they wouldn't.

11

When I got home, I called my sister. Every ring seemed like an eternity until I heard her voice.

"Ann?"

"Hi, Kris."

I skipped the formalities. I could barely talk, let alone chit-chat about the weather.

"Ann, I'm going to ask you one question, okay?" I said, out of breath.

"Sure, what is it?" She acted as if she were hurrying me along.

"Don't think about it, just answer, okay?" I instructed her.

"Okay, okay!"

"Your very first feeling," I commanded.

"What's the question? I'm on the other line —"

I blurted it out, "Do you think Dad ever molested us?"

Dead silence.

Then, "It's him on the other line, it's Dad," she said, no emotion in her voice.

"Oh, my God" was all I could say.

"I'll call you back," she said calmly.

"Soon!" I pleaded.

"Soon," she promised.

Gently, I put the phone back down on its receiver and waited in darkness for Ann's call.

What terrible timing. It wasn't surprising that Ann was talking to my dad. We both spoke to him several times a month.

After my parents' divorce ten years ago, he had changed. He mellowed. He started to treat each of us as individuals, not just as a gang of children. He remarried. Once lonely, he now seemed genuinely happy.

When the phone rang, after what seemed like an eternity but couldn't have been more than two minutes, I jumped.

It was Ann.

"Good Lord, Kris," she sounded mad.

"So what's your answer?" I asked, as if she were on trial.

"Sexually, you mean?"

"Yes," I said, feeling like I'd throw up.

"I don't know," she said, exasperated. "I don't think so."

I didn't believe her, because behind the exasperation, I heard fear in her voice, the same fear I felt in my stomach.

"Where did this come from?" Now, she sounded as if she were accusing me.

I told her everything I knew. About my dreams (although I couldn't bear to be explicit), about his fondness for bathing us and our inexplicable inability to swim, and about telling Destiny a few hours ago.

In the darkness of my apartment, my own words sounded feeble, even as I spoke them. I might not have believed them myself, except for the unmistakable proof: my rising nausea.

I excused myself from the phone, bolted to the bathroom, and barely made it to the toilet in time to throw up. It took me a while to find a clean washcloth. When I did, I wetted it, clamped it to my forehead, and picked up the phone again. My hands were shaking.

"Are you okay?" Ann asked.

"I think so. I just threw up."

"You never throw up."

"I know," I said weakly. "Maybe it was something I ate."

"It wasn't something you ate."

"I know," I said quietly.

"Do you want me to come over there? I could be there in a few minutes — just give me time to dress."

I looked around my living room. It was messier than normal: clothes, shoes, and remnants of meals long since forgotten dotted the plush carpet.

"Oh, God, no!" I exclaimed. I couldn't stand a housekeeping lecture from Ann, and I knew she'd give me one. I just knew it.

"You know I love the view, Kris. It wouldn't be any problem."

I looked out the window then, at Denver's skyline twinkling against a backdrop of blackness.

"Thanks anyway, Ann. Maybe we could just talk some more."

And talk we did. To her credit, although Ann wasn't sure my father had ever touched us inappropriately, she listened to my accusations. I listed all the logical clues that pointed to evidence of incest, though I never spoke the word out loud.

My father and mother had slept in separate bedrooms. Hers was upstairs, next to my little brother's and little sister's. His was downstairs, next to mine, across from Ann and Gail's. He had always walked around the house in his underwear. Jockey shorts, not boxer shorts. No robe. Everything quite visible.

As adults, Ann and I had watched his interactions with my sister Jill after he and my mother divorced. There had been an inordinate amount of affection between them. When Jill was sixteen, she had lain on the couch with her head in my father's lap, as my dad stroked her hair.

Ann and I talked until two o'clock that morning, a morning I'll never forget — the last day of winter.

When we hung up, I was so agitated, I knew I'd never sleep. Almost as if possessed, I put on my coat and went out.

One by one, I visited each of my family members' houses, sometimes sobbing so hard I could barely see to drive. First my mother's, the house I grew up in, the house where the abuse occurred. When I got there, my tears dried and my insides froze up. I sat there the longest, at the house that was no longer my home, the house that probably never had been.

I saw the basement window that looked into my father's old workroom. I remembered using one of his tools once, not to build, but to destroy. I had repeatedly hit my left thumb with his hammer. I did it slowly and carefully so that it didn't hurt too much. But I made sure that my thumb was bruised and swollen. I'm not sure why I bothered — no one in my family noticed the injury anyway.

I turned on the interior car light to look at my left thumb. It looked a little crooked. I tried to remember how old I was when I damaged it. I couldn't have been more than five years old then. Another memory from the first years of my life. No wonder I'd blocked them so well.

Next I went to my father's, the house that he shared with his new bride. There, I had no feelings. Absolutely nothing registered. I wanted to cry, to wash it all away.

Purify my body. Purify my soul. But I couldn't.

Where evil hands have touched, is a stain left?

This I wondered as I drove off.

In front of Ann's house, I cried a lot. For her and for me. Her lights were off — she must have gone to sleep after our phone call. I wondered if she was sleeping well.

Then, it was on to David's, the home he lived in with other chronically mentally ill people. David had been in and out of mental hospitals and boarding houses and even jail since he graduated from high school. Each year, his life seemed to get a little more desperate. Long ago, I'd started to deal with the fact that my brother would probably die at a very young age. Maybe from the effects of his epilepsy. Maybe from the effects of his depression. Maybe from the effects of my parents.

I would have visited Gail and Jill, too, but years earlier, they'd both fled to California.

So, I went home, my tour finished. Riding the elevator up to my apartment, I thought about the incredible highs and lows of the past twenty-four hours. How close they'd been to one another. The high of thinking Destiny had a crush on me — it had been a long time since I'd felt another woman's attraction to me. And the low of fully realizing the horror of what my father had done to me.

Life's bottom was really just the top turned upside down.

I looked at the clock before I turned out my bedroom light. It read four o'clock. Still, I tossed and turned for a long time before I finally fell asleep.

Someone in my bedroom.

I see a figure, large, hunched over, walking from my bed. Just his back.

Wearing loose-fitting underwear and a T-shirt. The underwear hangs on him exactly like my father's did.

The terror.

I willed myself awake.

CHAPTER

12

The phone rang just hours later as I walked into my office.
"Hey, Kris!"
"Destiny, hi! What are you doing?"
"Not much, pretending to work. How about you?"
"I just got in, but I'll start pretending pretty soon."
"Want to go to dinner tonight?"
I was both surprised and pleased at her invitation.
"I'd love to," I answered easily.
"Great. I'll come by and get you at seven."
"Okay. See you then."
"Not so fast, Kris. I really called to see how you're doing."
"Never been better," I lied.
"Really, are you okay?"
"I'm all right."
"Any regrets about telling me what you did?"
"It feels strange," I answered which was only partially true.
It felt more than strange. It felt wrong to have talked to
Destiny. Too sad. Too painful. Too incriminating.
Bill Ashe, my dad. He belonged to me. I belonged to him.
He was a horrible person. Or maybe he was an ordinary
person who had done horrible things, but he was all I had.
I wanted to tell Destiny all of this, but it seemed like further
betrayal. My own betrayal.
"Did you sleep well?"
I didn't answer.

"Kris, did you have one of those dreams?"

Still, I didn't answer.

"Kristin Ashe!" she shouted.

"Yes," I answered in a small voice. "But I can't talk about it right now, okay?"

"No, not okay!" Her vehemence shocked me. "We had a pact. Why didn't you call me? I've trusted you more than I've ever trusted anyone. Why can't you trust me?"

"I tried," I said lamely.

"What, and my line was busy, I suppose?"

"I tried, Destiny. Don't be angry. I just couldn't do it. I dialed the first six numbers of your phone number and then I hung up. I'm not playing games with you. I just couldn't do it," I said wearily.

"Really, you couldn't?" she asked in a much softer voice.

"Really. I wish I had called you — then maybe I could have gotten back to sleep. As it is, it's nine in the morning and I'm worn out. I can't do this much more," I said, and even I could hear the desperation in my voice.

"Work a little this morning, then nap this afternoon. Tonight after dinner, I'll come home with you and spend the night. That way, you won't have to call me. I'll be right there with you."

"Are you serious?" I was flabbergasted.

"Of course I am."

"You can't do that. You're dating Michelle."

"I'm not going to sleep on top of you. I'm just offering to stay over. Nothing sexual, I swear it."

"Nothing sexual?"

"Nothing sexual. Guaranteed."

For a minute, I was tempted. Very tempted.

Then good sense overcame me.

"Thanks anyway, Destiny, but I think I'd better sleep alone."

"All right, but you've got to swear you'll call next time."

"I'll call," I said without much conviction.

"Swear it, Kristin Ashe, or I'm packing my pajamas."

"I swear!" I said reluctantly and then added, "You really are stubborn, aren't you?"

"You betcha!"

"By the way, how are you this morning?"

"Never been better," was her bright, if sarcastic remark.

"Seriously," I prodded her.

"Seriously," her tone was now somber, "I'm okay. I feel a little weird, like last night was a night in someone else's life, but I'm okay. Better than I expected, actually."

"No regrets?"

"Not at all. Something's shifting in me, Kris. It's subtle and it's scary, and I'm not sure where it's all leading me to, but I'm ready to go."

"That's good. We'll keep going then," I said with perhaps more enthusiasm than I felt.

"Good, I'll see you tonight." And with that, she rang off.

• • •

When she picked me up, the first words out of her mouth were not flattering ones.

"You look terrible, Kris," she said as I opened the car door.

"Thanks, Destiny," I said without humor, pausing before I got into the car.

"Oh, no," she said, seeing that she'd hurt me, "I didn't mean it that way. You look tired, that's all. I can see you didn't sleep much."

"Everyone's been telling me I look awful. What is it exactly? I haven't broken out into zits. My hair isn't greasy. I brush and floss two times a day, sometimes three. What exactly is it that's changed?" I asked irritably.

"I guess I said the wrong thing?"

"You did, but seriously, what is it?"

She looked as if the last thing on earth she wanted to do was answer my question.

"C'mon, Destiny, what? Tell me and maybe I can change it."

"Okay, you asked for it. You have dark circles under your eyes and you frown a lot. You have a very deep frown line, you know, right between your eyes."

"I know, I've always had it. I was frowning as I came down the birth canal."

"You look a little pale, even your freckles look pale. Your nose is kind of red."

"I sunburned it yesterday on a bike ride," I said with a touch of hostility.

"The sun didn't come out yesterday, Kris, and you're the one who asked me to tell you this stuff. I think you look beautiful. You just don't look happy. Now will you please get in the car?"

"Okay," I conceded and dropped into the car seat. "Maybe I

shouldn't have put you on the spot like that. It's just that everyone's been telling me I look terrible, and I'm kind of tired of hearing it."

"Maybe they're concerned about you."

"Maybe," I grunted. "Where do you want to go to eat?"

"How about Italian?"

"Fine, I'm starved."

Destiny started the car but then abruptly shut off the engine.

"Maybe we shouldn't be doing this, Kris."

"Okay, we can go somewhere else. No problem. How about Mexican? There's a great new restaurant on Broadway."

"No, I'm not talking about food. I'm talking about our search. Maybe we should call it off."

"Why?" I asked, genuinely perplexed.

She looked away from me before she answered.

"I'm scared," was her quiet reply.

I reached over to comfort her.

"I'm here for you, Destiny. We can slow down, or even stop, if it's too much for you."

"It's not me, Kris." She paused. "I'm scared for you."

"Oh," I mumbled, withdrawing my hand from her shoulder.

"I'm scared about the effect it's having on you."

"I can manage," I said curtly.

"I know you can, but the question is, do you want to?"

I'd honestly never thought about it that way before. I'd simply coped. Even as a young child, I had elaborate defenses. On some level, I think I always knew I'd been abused. In reaction to the abuse, I'd treated my parents, and sometimes even my brothers and sisters, with the same hatred and scorn I'd learned.

I coped by pretending and what a good pretender I was. I pretended not to need the innocent, loving touch a child needs. I grew up not wanting anyone to touch me.

I pretended not to need the love and acceptance that never came from my parents. I grew up unable to fully accept the notion that anyone could love me.

I spent most of my life and much of my energy pretending not to need the most basic things a child needs. And when I became an adult, it didn't become any easier. Even though I was away from the abuse, I couldn't stop pretending. The pretense had become as much a part of me as my arms and legs.

For the first time, Destiny's question shone a whole new light on things. I could stop coping by telling myself lies every day and

90

start grieving the losses, the incredible losses that were my childhood.

"Yes, I want to keep going, Destiny."

There was silence.

"I had to ask, Kris. I hope I didn't offend you," Destiny said gently.

"You didn't," I muttered.

"Good. Then while I'm on a roll, could I ask just one more question?"

"Sure," I sighed.

"Can we eat Chinese? I'm not in the mood for Italian anymore," she said apologetically.

"Of course." I smiled and shook my head in disbelief.

Over a delicious meal of sesame chicken and lemon scallops, we chatted easily about everything under the sun except our families. After the dishes were cleared, she told me she'd called her father that day to tell him about her visit with her biological grandmother.

"What did he say?" I was astounded she'd had the courage to talk to him so soon, to bring her two lives together.

"Not much. He was surprised I'd met her. He asked a few questions about her."

"Did he seem supportive?"

She thought for a moment.

"I think he wants to be supportive, but it's hard for him, especially with my mom calling him every other day."

"I thought they didn't speak to each other — that's the impression I got from him."

"They don't usually. My search seems to have brought them together. Isn't that ironic?"

"You're kidding!"

"I'm not."

"What's your mom's reaction?"

"She's flipped her lid, according to my dad. She used to call me practically every day, but she hasn't called since I told her I was looking for my family. That's her way of showing me she's angry. According to my dad, she calls him all the time to get updates. It's sickening!"

"Do you think your mom's scared of what you might find out?"

"I don't honestly know what her problem is. My dad didn't react this way when I told him what I planned to do. I can't imagine why this is affecting her like it is. We aren't even close."

"Maybe that's the problem."

"I'm sure it is, but it's been a problem for twenty-five years. She and I have never been close. Maybe that's part of why I'm looking for my real mother, to find out more about the mom I was close to."

"That's probably what your mom's afraid of."

"Well, I can't put my whole life on hold because of her fears, because my healing process might hurt her," Destiny said with enough anger to make me feel uncomfortable.

"Of course, you can't. I'm not suggesting that. But maybe you could talk to her directly about what you're doing, instead of having her find out from your father."

"She could call herself if she's so curious," the little warrior retorted.

"Are you scared of her?"

"Sure I am, who isn't scared of her mother?"

"Good point. I'm terrified of mine."

"Have you talked to her about what you're going through, Kris, about your dreams and stuff?"

"Oh, God, no!" I laughed without mirth at the thought. "I haven't talked to her about anything in over two years, much less about, ahm, incest." God, the power of that word — incest. Saying it was at once freeing and binding.

"Two years?"

"Yep," I said, almost proudly.

"Why not?"

It was hard to explain.

I thought for a long time before I answered her.

"When I was younger, I resented her for the control she had over our family, that we were all influenced by the way she felt on a given day. In her craziness, she made me feel crazy, too. And you know, Destiny, I don't think she ever liked me. Not from the day I was born. When I was in high school, I knew she hated me and the feeling was mutual. I left for college without saying good-bye to her.

"When I came back after a year of school, I tried to have a relationship with her, but it was so draining. Finally, I got tired of it. Of all the phone conversations where she talked for an hour and I talked for a minute. Of all the holidays she ruined by refusing to get out of bed. When I was a kid, I had no choice. I had to be around her emotional abuse and her mental illness. As an adult, I have a choice. Not an easy one, but at least a choice."

"Do you think she's truly ill?"

I nodded my head.

"I begged her to get help. When I first started my business, and I was only making eight hundred dollars a month, I offered to pay for counseling for her. She wouldn't go. She insisted that our family was sick, not her. To this day, I agree with her — our family is sick, every last one of us. But so is she."

"Do you have any contact with her now?"

"Not if I can help it," I said adamantly. "One month she sends me a nice birthday card, saying she misses me. The next month, she sends me my vaccination papers — like she's trying to get every trace of me out of her house. I mean, what do I need twenty-year-old vaccination papers for now?"

"Does your sister stay in touch with her?"

"Ann?"

Destiny nodded.

"No, she stopped talking to her around the same time I did but for different reasons. I can't even remember what they were anymore. My other sisters, Gail and Jill, both live in California. I think they moved there to get away from my family, but the distance allows them to think they have good relationships with both my mother and father. I'm sure my father molested Gail. There's no way he couldn't have. In age, she's right between me and Ann. Maybe he molested David, too. As for Jill, I'm not sure about her. I'd hate to even know. I was seven years older than her, and I tried so hard to protect her."

"How sad!"

"I've thrown away most of the things my parents have given me over the years, what few there were," I said matter-of-factly.

"But don't you miss your mom?"

"Not really," I answered a fraction too quickly. "Well, maybe that's not true. I guess I do miss her a little, and I probably always will. Mostly, I miss the idea of a mother, of someone she's never been. I don't even tell people anymore that I live in the same city as her but never see her. They always suggest I reconcile, as if there's been some mild misunderstanding. I've tried, Destiny. God knows, I've tried. But what I really need to do, the much harder thing to do, is reconcile myself to the fact that the mother I have will never treat me in a loving, respectful way. And so, I can't be around her. That's what I regret. I don't regret not being around her the way she is."

We were both quiet, sitting in an awkward silence. Ready to

pay the bill, I searched for the waiter.

"How often do you see your dad, Kris?" Destiny asked me in a quiet voice.

My attention snapped back to her. I laughed a bitter laugh.

"Ironically, I see him quite often. The last time I saw him was just before I met you. We went out to dinner."

"Will you see him again now that you know what he did?"

"I'm not sure — I haven't really thought that far ahead."

"I couldn't see him."

"Sure you could."

She looked at me strangely.

"Your coping skills are as fine-tuned as mine. I can block out the abuse, Destiny. I can separate the man he is today from the man he was then. At great cost to myself, but I can do it. Completely. Just like I've done all my life. Just like you did last night at your grandma's, until she called you 'little one.' "

"Then I lost it," she admitted, a bit embarrassed.

"But you got control of yourself again."

"Aren't you ever afraid you'll lose it for good, Kris? That something will trigger it, and all the memories will come flooding back at once, and you won't be able to endure the pain?"

"I'm afraid of that all the time. Ready for it, yet deathly afraid of it."

How could I not be afraid? I'd read books and articles and newspaper stories about other women who were the victims of incest. Their lives were often pictures of childhood abuse turned into adult tragedy. Women who lost everything: their jobs, their sanity, even their lives, when the memories returned.

I took three quick sips from my water glass.

"This may seem like a dumb question, but then why would you want to see your father?"

I smiled half-heartedly. "This may seem like a dumb answer, but I can't bear to lose both my mother and my father. For the last ten years, beginning when he and my mom divorced, I've really liked him. He's been supportive of my work, he's acknowledged my lovers, and he's treated me with kindness and respect. My mom's abuse, I clearly remember — in excruciating detail — when I'm awake. His abuses, so far, I only remember — in vague imagery — when I'm asleep. Each day, I try to put it all behind me, to focus on the life I have now. Most days I succeed. Some, I don't. There have been times recently when I've been afraid I'd crack under the pressure of keeping it all together, or separate rather. Today, everything in my world seems different than it did yesterday, but for the first time in a long time, I don't feel crazy."

"Do you think your mother knows your father abused you and your sisters?"

Even though I'd already given that question hours of consideration, it took me a minute to answer.

"I think so, on some level." I breathed deeply. "I think that may have been part of what drove her to her bed. She's so bitter today, and half of what makes her bitter is that we all have a relationship with my father. It infuriates her because she believes we think she's the only sick one. It's almost like she's been on the verge of telling us that his sickness dwarfs hers, but she never could quite seem to find the words. Because to find the words, she'd have to admit that she knew what was going on.

"The main difference between my parents, Destiny, is that my mom has carried my father's guilt. But he has never carried hers. I'm sure that he doesn't waste one minute of his life today worrying that perhaps he should have done something more for his children when his wife took to her bed for years on end."

"What did he do?"

"He golfed. He drank thirty-five thousand beers — and I'm not exaggerating. I figured that out one day. He let us fend for ourselves. Now pretend that she *did* know something was going on, and again, I'm not sure that she did, but pretend that she did. What did she do? She became so depressed that she couldn't get up. That's the difference between the two of them. He feels nothing. And she feels too much."

"I don't know how you do it, Kris."

"Do what?"

"I don't know how you manage to live without feeling rage every day of your life, rage at these two people who did these horrible things to you."

"I don't. I try to control my rage, but it's always there."

Destiny reached over to calm my hands that were playing with packs of sugar as if they were cards.

"This means a lot that you're talking to me, Kris."

"About my family?" I stopped fiddling.

"About yourself."

"Thanks for listening." I smiled at her shyly. She grinned.

Right then, at that exact moment, I realized that for the first time in my life, I had a true friend. It made me sad for all the years I'd spent alone, for all the time I'd lost.

Destiny must have seen the frown cross my forehead.

"Hey, Kris, why the frown? What's wrong?"

"Nothing," I said, erasing the sorrow. "Let's talk about you for a minute. My next plan is to meet with Lydia Barton — your mom's old friend...."

CHAPTER

13

The next Saturday, with a twinge of guilt, I realized it had been a long time since I'd talked to my grandma.

Pretending to be on my way home from the library, I stopped by her house to see if she needed any groceries.

As independent as Grandma Ashe was, she'd never learned to drive a car. Once, I'd gotten her to take a spin around the block on my moped, but that was the extent of her motoring experience.

Whenever I could, I stopped by to take her grocery shopping. I rarely needed groceries myself because I never ate at home, but I didn't mind taking her.

I rang the doorbell several times but got no answer. Undaunted, I peered in the front window and spotted Grandma sitting comfortably oblivious in her living room. By banging on the screen and jumping up and down, I finally got her attention.

We met at the front door.

"Hi, honey, why didn't you ring the bell?" She hugged me.

"I did," I said, suppressing my irritation. "Maybe your hearing aids aren't working, Grandma," I added, although I could see full well she wasn't wearing them.

"Oh, I only wear them when I have company. I'll go get them." She retreated into the bedroom.

When she left the room, I walked over to her mantle and studied the family pictures I'd seen a hundred times before. This time was different, though. This time, I was looking for clues.

There were my cousins in long hair and bell bottoms, and there was my grandpa, a man who died before I was born.

And there was our family. Father, mother, four girls and a boy. Even then, even when we were all together, we looked miserable, especially me. My body language told it all. In every picture, I was standing a good foot away from everyone else, looking perpetually mad. Forever, I had tried to separate.

My grandma returned, hearing aids in place.

"Do you think Mom and Dad were good parents, Grandma?"

She looked at me quizzically, like I'd grown two heads while she was out of the room, and for a second, I thought she wasn't going to answer.

"They did their best, honey. That's all anyone can do."

"But do you think their best was good enough?"

"That's not for us to decide," she said in a conversation-ending tone. I knew I'd pushed her too far, but I couldn't help myself. I couldn't keep pretending, even though I knew that's exactly what she wanted me to do.

She handed me several sheets of paper she'd brought from the kitchen. They were coupons, and they returned us to the safety of our superficial rituals. She always gave me coupons to restaurants; I always pretended to use them but instead threw them away when I got home.

"Here's a two-for-one at Gino's. And another one for Maxi's, but it expires this week. I haven't seen you in a while, you know," she delivered a mild reprimand.

"I've been busy —" I started to explain.

"And you're not looking good, Kristin," she interrupted me.

Just once, just one measly time, I wished someone would tell me I looked good.

"Are you getting enough sleep?"

"No," I admitted.

"You work too hard. You always have. You should try to get to bed early."

"I will," I said feebly.

I didn't bother telling her that I often went to bed early, but dream terrors woke me. Dreams of my father, her son, attacking me.

"I was just on my way to the grocery store, do you need anything?"

"I could use a few things. Let me get my list."

Minutes after we arrived at the store, I was done with my

shopping. My purchases were a *People* magazine and an ice cold Dr. Pepper.

I went back out to the car to wait for Grandma.

If Grandma ever noticed that I didn't really need to go to the store, she never mentioned it. We Ashe girls were less than honest sometimes; she pretended not to need me, and I pretended not to be as kind as I was.

I was halfway through the week's gossip when a car pulled up next to mine. A late model Chevrolet Celebrity. Out of it stepped two young girls, about high school age, and from the back seat sprang a little boy, about seven years of age. One of the girls put her arm around the kid's shoulder and the three of them walked into the store together. There was a lightness to their steps. I wanted to run and catch up with them and ask if I could spend the rest of the day doing whatever they were doing. But I didn't.

Instead, I put down the magazine, reclined in my seat, took off my glasses and closed my eyes as the sun came through the car windows and warmed my body.

I thought about Grandma's answer to the question of whether my parents were good parents. She had said "That's not for us to decide," but she was wrong. It was for me to decide. I thought about all the ways and all the days I'd tried, in vain, to get my parents' attention.

I rubbed the area on my nose where my eyeglasses had just been and thought about how I'd gotten my first pair of glasses. In an effort to get my parents' attention, I "cheated" on the eye exam. I pretended to not see letters that I saw. The next thing I knew, I had glasses. I kept thinking someone would catch me at some point, that they'd discover I was faking. But they never did. At the age of twenty-nine, my eyesight was genuinely limited. I wondered if it was then... when I was six years old and freshly bespectacled. It was funny, the things I'd forgotten. It felt odd to have the memories returning in such strange, strange sequences.

After what seemed like three days, Grandma finally came out of the store, slowly pushing her cart. Usually, I hopped right out and ran to help her. But this time, I froze. From a safe distance, I watched her and I thought about what it would be like to speak the truth, to tell her what my life was really like.

It would kill her, the thought occurred to me. The truth would kill her.

But what was the silence doing to me?

Unwilling to answer that question, I sprinted over to help her. Together, each of our hands clasping the bar, we pushed the cart back to the car.

Once there, I tossed aside the croquet set and tennis rackets and cleared a space in the back of my Honda for her groceries. I unloaded the six bags, my grandma's idea of "a few things," and we were off.

We had the most inane conversation during our short journey back to her house.

"I saw Alberta Balkenbush today. You remember Alberta...."

"Er, no." I rarely met any of the friends she talked about, but that never stopped her from thinking I knew them.

"She has cancer now. She lost her leg. Had it cut off right here."

I think she pointed to the area where the thigh meets the hip, but I couldn't be sure since I was trying to keep my eyes on the road.

"Mmm."

"She's got an artificial leg now. Two actually."

"She lost both legs?" I was horrified, even if I didn't know her.

"No, one for high heels and one for low heels. Spent two thousand dollars."

"For both?"

"No, each!" she said, the judgment apparent in her voice.

"No kidding!"

"Can you imagine that?"

"No, I can't, Grandma. I simply cannot."

She slowly nodded her head, her lips turned downward.

Well, there wasn't much more to say after that, so we drove the rest of the way in silence. When we got to Grandma's house, I carried in her groceries and then hugged her, promising I'd stop in again soon. I barely heard her last words, spoken as the screen door slammed shut.

"Life's good if you don't weaken," she called out, and I knew exactly what she meant.

It was the Ashe credo. Don't ever let anyone see that something's bothering you. Or better yet, don't let anything bother you. I'd lived most of my life by those words, and they'd served me well. But I'd outlived the words' function. It was time for me to weaken. I'd missed out on too many things by not weakening.

I'd like to say that I went back inside and explained all this to Grandma, but I didn't. I simply got in my car and drove home.

On the early evening news, the lead story was about, of all things, artificial limbs. Earlier in the day, someone had broken into Denver Prosthetics and stolen all the arms and legs. At that hour, the police had no suspects, and not surprisingly, no motives.

I hoped they hadn't gotten Alberta's leg. Either one of them.

I went to see a French movie at the Ogden theater, came home, finished off the *People* magazine and then almost instantly fell into a deep sleep.

I dreamed, but not the usual dreams. I dreamed I found the stolen arms and legs on top of a Volkswagen camper. I was a hero for returning the missing parts of so many people.

CHAPTER

14

The next morning, I was rudely awakened by the ringing phone. I couldn't believe how loud it sounded.

"Hello," I mumbled, fumbling to look at the clock. It was 8:30.

"Kris, hi! I'm glad I caught you before you went out," the familiar voice chirped.

"Hi, Michelle," I grumbled. "You know good and well I won't be going anywhere for several hours. It's Sunday. I had intended to sleep. What's up?"

"Not much. I've been reading the paper this morning and playing with my cats. Speaking of which, did I tell you about the cute veterinarian I met the other day? I think I'm going to start taking my cats to her."

"No, you didn't, and I don't want to hear about her now. Why did you call me at the crack of dawn?"

"Actually, Kris, the crack of dawn was hours ago, plus —" she started to protest.

"Michelle, what is it?" I practically shouted.

"I need to talk to you. Can you meet me at the Botanic Gardens in an hour? I'll bring breakfast."

"I'll be there," I sighed.

This was serious! The Botanic Gardens was Michelle's favorite place to express sorrow. That was my first clue something was amiss. My second one came with her rare offer to bring food. For some reason, she always expected me to pick up the snacks.

"I'll see you in an hour, Kris."

"Okay."

"Don't be late."

"I won't," I promised as I set my alarm to capture another half hour of glorious sleep.

"It's about Destiny. 'Bye!" She wisely clicked off before I could conjure up a response.

Well, that did it! Now I was wide awake. What was going on? Did she have more psychic clues to offer me, clues which I'd have to pretend to take seriously? Or was there something wrong between her and Destiny?

I could see the answer in Michelle's face when we met at the front gate of the Gardens. She looked like she'd been crying for weeks.

"You look awful," I said, perhaps somewhat in spite because everyone had been saying it to me.

"I feel awful. That's why I look awful."

We paid to get in and headed straight for her favorite pond.

"Here," she thrust the box of donuts at me as soon as we were seated. "I'm not hungry."

"I'm not *that* hungry," I said eyeing the dozen donuts.

"Eat as many as you want. I'll take the rest home."

"Okay." I bit into a maple donut and settled in on the bench overlooking the pond.

"Destiny and I aren't seeing each other anymore," she said as I started to chew.

I choked on my donut.

I shouldn't have been shocked but I was. Not even so much because their relationship had ended, but because Destiny hadn't said a word to me.

"Whose decision was it?"

"Destiny's, but she's trying to convince me it's mutual."

"What happened?"

"She came over last night and told me it was over. She said she couldn't go on like we'd been — in a fun, superficial relationship with no strings attached — and that she wasn't ready for a more serious relationship."

"Huh."

"I ask you, Kris," Michelle said, dabbing at her nearly dry eyes with a Kleenex, "What's wrong with fun and superficial? I'd have liked more, or at least I think I would have, but I accepted that she couldn't give more. I just wanted to spend time with her. I didn't care what we called it."

I didn't say anything.

"What's going on, Kris? Ever since you started helping her find her family, she's changed. I can't put my finger on it, but she's different." Michelle attacked me with her words.

"I can't talk to you about Destiny, Michelle. Can't you ask her yourself?"

"I did, but I still don't get it. I've been going crazy trying to guess what I did wrong."

"I'm sure you didn't do anything wrong."

"Then please, Kris, I beg of you, tell me what's going on."

Because her dramatics at the pond were beginning to draw attention from a gaggle of elderly women admiring a nearby flowerbed, and also because I couldn't resist the pain in her voice, I started to talk.

"Destiny's been going through some rough stuff lately. Has she told you about any of it?"

She shook her head.

Great!

"Well, I can't either. I wish I could, but I can't violate her trust. All I can say is that it's terribly hard and no human being who had any feelings at all could remain unchanged by what she's discovering."

"It's that bad?" Michelle asked meekly.

I nodded.

"I never knew. I thought it was about me. She never tells me anything."

"No offense, Michelle, but in the whole scheme of things, you're a very small part of Destiny's life right now."

"Too small, I guess."

"Probably."

"Maybe that's why she broke up with me. That's kind of what she said last night."

"Maybe."

"Thanks, Kris."

"For what?" I asked. I already felt bad enough — both about what I'd said and what I'd withheld — without her thanking me.

"For being my friend."

"You're welcome," I said, feeling even more guilty.

I'd always been Michelle's friend, but really, I had never let her be mine. For years, we'd shared meals and friends and activities, but I'd never really shared myself. Not the deepest, darkest parts. Not the parts I'd shared with Destiny.

I'd let Michelle lean on me, but I had never trusted her enough to lean back. Partially, I distrusted her because she always acted so frivolous and carefree. I wasn't sure she'd understand my true despair, because she never seemed to feel much herself.

If I knew her, she'd be over Destiny in a week, two at the most. I felt bad for her and yet at the same time, happy for myself. Destiny and I had found each other, and it was a miracle. A miracle Michelle would never comprehend.

We were both silent awhile. I busied myself staring at my reflection in the Japanese pond.

"How did you leave things with her?" I finally spoke when the silence became uncomfortable.

"What else — we'll be friends. The story of my life," Michelle said without bitterness.

"Maybe you can see each other again when this is all over," I suggested, though I doubted it.

"Maybe," Michelle's tone echoed my doubt. "In the meantime, I think I'll schedule an appointment with that cute vet."

"Is one of your cats sick?"

"No, but an extra set of vaccinations probably wouldn't hurt them, would it?"

"I don't have the foggiest. For all I know, it could kill them." I hoped the disgust didn't show in my voice. "Maybe you should check first."

"Maybe you could call Gallagher and ask her," she suggested because she knew Gallagher made her living in Provincetown as a veterinary technician.

"Nice try, Michelle. I'm not going to call Gallagher. You've got her number, call her yourself if you're that concerned." Sometimes, Michelle's insensitivity galled me.

I plucked a glazed donut from the box and took a huge bite out of it, marvelling at Michelle's bionic heart, capable of erasing women from her memory in a single night. When she spoke, her words diluted some of my scorn.

"I'll miss her, Kris."

There was nothing I could say to that. I kept on chewing.

CHAPTER

15

The next day, I left work early to meet Lydia Barton, the woman who had been Barbara Kenwood's best friend. When I'd called ahead to set up the appointment, I could tell this woman wasn't thrilled to talk to me, but perhaps out of deference to Marie Kenwood, she invited me to her home.

Lydia Barton was a realtor, and by the looks of it, a successful one. Her home in the Denver Country Club had the requisite Mercedes, license plate RLTR, in the driveway.

She came to the door in a business suit, every bottle-black hair in place. She wore an expensive gold watch on her wrist and several diamonds on her fingers, though none in the matrimonial place. Her bifocal glasses hung from a chain around her neck.

She hated to be called Mrs. Barton. The name reminded her of a husband who had left her some years ago for a younger woman. Her only daughter, Janine, who was Destiny's age, lived in San Francisco with a woman electrician who was her "best friend." All of this, and much more, Lydia Barton told me before we had a chance to sit down.

It was going to be a long afternoon, I thought, as I struggled to listen to Lydia Barton's high pitched, fast-paced monologue.

The tape recorder made things even worse. When I asked permission to record our conversation, she immediately gave it, then performed as if she were on stage.

"Barb Kenwood was a lovely woman, just lovely, and Pete, he

was always the gentleman, always the gentleman. Tragic, their story's so tragic. Struck down in the prime of their lives, the very prime."

At this rate, with her repeating everything, we'd need two days for the interview.

I checked my impatience and asked, "How well did you know the Kenwoods?"

"Barb and I were like sisters. She was such a dear friend."

"You met when you moved in next door to the Kenwoods, isn't that right?"

"Oh, that Marie, she must have told you everything. What a dear woman. Isn't she a dear?"

"She's a peach," I said without a trace of sarcasm, I swear it. God help me, I was starting to adopt Lydia's lingo.

"She's such a lovely woman. No one loved Destiny more than she. Or loved Pete more either. She was devastated by the loss. We all were, of course, but she suffered the most. Pete was her whole life. She'd lost her husband to cancer the year before, you know," she said conspiratorially.

"Yes," I said, trying to look sufficiently sympathetic. "Are you and Mrs. Kenwood close now?"

"Oh, no! She won't allow it. We were before the accident. Dick and I — Dick's my ex-husband — we always invited her to our backyard barbecues, our little gatherings. She'd return the courtesy by inviting us to her house for cards. She plays a mean hand of poker for a lady. Me, I never particularly cared for the game, but I'd go along with the gang."

"I'll *bet* she's a good poker player," I said.

"She intimidated you, didn't she?" Lydia asked, smiling almost spitefully, as if she knew everything about my first meeting with Destiny's grandmother.

"A little, at first," I admitted sheepishly.

"She's like that. I was scared to death of her when I met her. Fortunately, she softened up quite a bit after Destiny came along. Destiny brought out something in her. She adored that child, simply adored her."

"So you lost touch with Mrs. Kenwood after Barbara and Peter died?"

"Oh, no, nothing like that. We've always been in touch. Every Christmas and every Easter, we send one another cards. We just haven't seen each other in twenty-five years."

"Why not?"

"That's how she wanted it, and I respected her wishes. After Barb and Pete died, she took it so hard. I stopped over to see her, to try to offer her my condolences, but she'd have no part of it. I couldn't utter their names in front of her, or Destiny's either. Once, when I stopped in to see her, Janine, my little girl, was with me. Marie couldn't even look at poor Janine. That was after she'd lost Destiny, too. I could tell my visits were hard on her, so I quit stopping by her house and she never called. Not until last week, that is."

"Were Mrs. Kenwood and Barbara close?"

She laughed.

"Not exactly. She didn't like Barb at first. No one was good enough for her Pete. Then, when she found out Barb's family thought Pete wasn't good enough for their daughter, that really rankled her. Barb used to tell me stories about how cold she was at first, but bless her heart, Barb wore her down with kindness. She had a way with people, Barb did. She was the sweetest person you could hope to meet. The day Dick and I moved in, Barb and Pete came over to welcome us to the neighborhood, and darned if she wasn't carrying a casserole. Dick thought it was corny, but I was touched by the gesture. They were such a cute couple, so in love. Dick made fun of how lovey-dovey they were together."

"Were Peter and your husband good friends."

"If you mean did they lend each other tools and share an occasional beer on the patio like all men do, then yes. If you mean were they best friends, no. Dick was too obnoxious for a cultured man like Pete."

She reached into the crystal candy dish in front of her, picked up a mint, and delicately put it on her tongue. She passed the dish to me but I declined.

As she sucked on the mint, a pensive frown crossed her face.

"Pete was a quiet man who kept to himself. He was quite enchanting when you could get him to talk, but he was extremely shy. He and Barb complemented each other in that way, because she was so outgoing, such a ball of fire. My husband was loud and crass. He drank too much and said things he shouldn't have. Pete loved chess and the symphony. Dick loved football and himself."

"Hmm," was all I said, though I was tempted to ask if she wished she'd married Peter instead of Dick. Clearly, the remnants of a strong crush were still there, all these years later.

"The two of them only did things together when Barb and I dragged them along. They put up with each other, but I wouldn't call them friends."

"What did the four of you do together?"

"Before the girls came along, we played pinochle every Friday night. Pete and I were partners and, if I do say so myself, we made a pretty good team. Dick and I started out as partners, but we fought too much. Pete had more patience with me."

"Did you see much of the Kenwoods after the girls were born?"

"Not as couples, but Barb and I became closer. The girls changed our lives, that's for sure. We saw each other almost every day. We'd talk about formulas and diapers and clothes. I dare say I couldn't have made it through those first months of motherhood without Barb. She was a saint, truly a saint."

"You both stayed home to raise the girls?"

"Yes, and it almost drove us crazy." She laughed. "Barb had been a nurse, and she missed her job at the hospital and her friends. I'd worked as a secretary for Dick's construction company, so I was glad for the change. Never work for your husband," she advised.

"Don't worry," I said, smiling.

"Being mothers was quite an adjustment for both of us."

"Were Destiny and Janine good friends?"

She rolled her eyes and smiled fondly.

"They were inseparable. Dick said they were like twins. He used to kid Pete that he was Destiny's real father. I personally found his humor to be in very poor taste, but that was Dick. The girls even developed their own language," she added proudly.

"You're kidding!" I was impressed.

"Before they started talking to any of us, they were talking to themselves, in a language none of us could understand. Barb and I thought they were geniuses. Sometimes, for kicks, we'd put them in Barb's living room and hide behind the couch and watch them play. We were spying on them when Destiny spoke her first real word. And you know what that was?" she asked, her voice bursting with pride.

I wanted to guess "Janine" but didn't. I shook my head.

" 'Nene.' That was her first word. She never did learn to say Janine."

"What was Janine's first word?" I asked, hoping it would be some derivative of Destiny. No such luck.

"Mama."

110

Of course. I should have known.

"It must have been hard on Janine when Destiny left?"

"It was terribly hard on her, poor thing. Every day for months, she asked if she could go to Destiny's house to play. Every day, I had to explain to her that Barb and Pete were gone and Destiny was with her new family. Twice, I called the church to see if we could go see Destiny — for both the girls' sake. I wanted to show Janine that Destiny was all right and I'm sure a visit from us would have done Destiny a world of good, a world of good. Both times, those nasty nuns flatly turned me down. Try explaining that to a four-year-old."

"Did you see Destiny at all after the accident?"

"Only once. Marie let her come over one night to say good-bye to Janine. That was their last night together. Of course, we both knew it, but neither one of us could bring ourselves to tell them. I think they sensed it, though. They played 'house' all night long, like they always did, but when I looked in on them later when they were sleeping, I knew they knew. They were lying side by side in Janine's bed, holding hands. The sight of them made me burst into tears. I'd lost my best friend, and my little girl was losing hers. We never saw Destiny again, and Janine never had another best friend — until recently. She lives with her friend now, and I'm glad for her. After Destiny, she never showed much interest in having friends."

"Can you tell me what Destiny was like as a little girl?"

"Oh, she was a feisty one. She had her father's brains and her mother's drive. She was always asking questions, questions there were rarely answers to. She drove Barb crazy with all her questions, and Barb, God love her, patiently answered them all. I would have swatted her a few times, but Barb never did."

"When would you have done that?"

"The time she ate breakfast in her birthday suit, for one."

"You're kidding!" I laughed.

"I'm not! One morning after she'd spent the night here, I called the girls down for breakfast. Barb was here — she'd come over for coffee. Well, that Destiny, darned if she didn't come downstairs naked. I tell you, she had absolutely nothing on, and she announced she was ready for breakfast. Barb told her she'd have to go upstairs and get dressed first, but that ornery Destiny hopped up on a chair and refused to budge. She was going to eat breakfast just like that, thank you, ma'am."

Lydia paused to muffle a fake chuckle.

111

"Well, Barb was already running late for an appointment so she didn't have time to argue with her, plus she was laughing too hard. Janine, never one to be outdone, took her clothes off and joined her. I left my robe on, Barb left her dress on, and the four of us ate breakfast. The girls couldn't have been more than two-and-a-half years old then. After we were done eating, Destiny obediently put her clothes on, and Barb told me she never again ate naked. I don't know what got into her, but there was no stopping her when she got an idea into her head. It was a waste of time to even try to change her mind."

"It sounds like Barbara was a good mother."

"The best! She was wonderful. She loved to teach her things. She'd explain them to her step by step, and she had to. Destiny wouldn't rest until she had the answers. This may sound odd, but I think Barb appreciated Destiny more than most mothers appreciate their children. She was their gift. They thought they'd never be able to have children, and then Destiny came into their lives. That's why they chose that name. It was Barb's idea to call her Destiny because she thought she was so special. And she was. I missed seeing her grow up. What is she like now, can you tell me?"

I started to tell her about the grown-up Destiny Greaves when the phone rang. Lydia Barton got up to answer it.

While she was gone, I took the liberty of looking around the room. Inside a very large green lacquer entertainment center, I saw the latest in electronics and some family photos. I made a beeline for the pictures.

It seemed like there were hundreds, all of them of the same person, who I could only surmise was Janine. She'd been an adorable baby, a very cute kid, and she wasn't a bad looking woman. Her newborn picture showed a full head of dark hair. Her first school picture showed that same thick hair bobbed and bowed. Now, I noted with approval, she had a short cut that accented her strong facial features and dark complexion. In one picture, she and another woman, the "best friend" I guessed, were standing quite close. Just as I suspected!

From the other room, I could hear bits and pieces of Lydia's conversation. If I understood correctly, Lydia was about to lose a very large deal because the clients were developing buyer's remorse. When she came back into the room, she apologized for having to cut our time short and said she had an emergency.

She showed me to the door, and almost as an afterthought,

said, "What a tragic life Destiny's had, losing two mothers at such a young age."

"I'm sure you were as much a mother to her as Barbara was."

"Not me. Destiny's other mother — her real mother," she corrected me.

"But Liz Greaves isn't dead," I protested. "True, they don't have a close relationship, but she hasn't lost her."

"Not the Greaves woman," she said impatiently. "Her real mother, the young woman who put her up for adoption."

I stopped dead in my tracks on the threshold. I felt like someone had hit me in the stomach.

"What woman? I'm not following you," I said, although I was beginning to suspect a horrible twist to Destiny's life story.

"Marie Kenwood didn't tell you?" she asked, panicked by her own admission.

"Tell me what?"

"I really must be going. Thanks for stopping by...." she said hurriedly and started to close the door.

I gently blocked the closing door with my hand, hoping she wouldn't slam it.

"Tell me what, Mrs. Barton?"

"I thought you knew, or I wouldn't have said anything."

"Knew *what*?" I was beginning to get exasperated.

Seeing that I wasn't going away any time soon and that as each second ticked by, she was risking the loss of her precious commission, she let out a heavy sigh and told me the astounding truth.

"I thought you knew Destiny was adopted."

I did and I didn't.

"By Barbara and Peter?"

"Yes. They couldn't have children of their own and they adopted Destiny."

"How old was she when they got her?"

"Two or three days old, maybe a week," she said, clearly not wanting to answer my questions.

"Do you know anything about the mother who gave her up?"

"No, except Barb told me she almost didn't give the baby up," she said as she looked at her Cartier wristwatch. "Excuse me, but I really must be going."

"Could I call you later?"

"I wish you wouldn't. I shouldn't have said anything. All of this was a long time ago, a very long time ago," she said, closing the door another inch.

"Please, for Destiny's sake? She might want to see Janine."

"I don't think that would be a good idea. My daughter was very hurt when Destiny left."

"So was Destiny. She still is."

"All right. The next time I talk to Janine, I'll tell her you stopped by. She's a grown woman, she can make her own decisions. But I really must run now."

With that, she shut the door tightly.

Driving away, I pondered what on earth I'd say to Destiny. I knew about three of her mothers so far, two more than most of us were burdened with. What more could go wrong? I shouldn't have asked. The possibilities were endless.

CHAPTER

16

Without my usual careful thought, which was probably just as well, I drove straight to Marie Kenwood's home. All the way across town, I seethed. I couldn't believe she hadn't had the decency to tell me Destiny was adopted. I was mad as hell and ready to confront her.

I screeched into her driveway and scraped a sculpted bush. Just as well. I hated sculpted bushes. I burst from my car and marched up the sidewalk.

Foregoing the bell, I banged on her door. Soon, I heard shuffling, saw the curtain move, and at last felt the door open.

In my fury, I wasn't prepared for how glad she would be to see me. All of her brusqueness from our earlier visits was gone. She greeted me like I was a long-lost friend.

"Kristin, what a surprise! How nice it is to see you!"

"Hello, Mrs. Kenwood," I said gruffly.

"What's wrong, dear, you don't look good."

"I don't feel good. May I come in?"

"Certainly. I was getting ready to make myself a bite to eat, but that can wait. How are you, young lady?"

"I just came from Lydia Barton's."

Marie Kenwood brightened visibly.

"How nice for you. Did you enjoy your time with her?" She led me into the living room, sat down on the couch, and gestured for me to join her.

I ignored her question and remained standing.

"Let's cut the niceties, Mrs. Kenwood. Lydia told me Destiny was adopted. Peter and Barbara weren't her real parents, and you're not her grandmother."

If I'd slapped her as hard as I could, it couldn't have hurt her more. Her face turned ashen white. She began fumbling with her knitting which sat next to her on the couch.

"I was going to tell you...." she stammered.

"When?" I barked.

"As soon as I could. I tried to tell you the night you were both here, but I didn't have the heart. It was such an enjoyable evening. I'd missed Destiny so much. I didn't want anything to interfere with our time together."

"What about before? Why didn't you tell me the first time I met you? You didn't have anything to lose then?"

"When you called me on the phone, I thought you knew. You said you'd been to see Benjamin Greaves. I presumed he told you. When you came to see me, I thought you'd bring it up if you wanted to talk about it. When you didn't, I didn't. Only much later did I realize you didn't know."

"You should have told me then."

By that point, she'd had enough of my anger. She lashed back at me with years worth of her own.

"Wasn't there enough tragedy already? How dare you judge me! Barbara may not have given birth to Destiny and it's true my son wasn't her 'real' father, but she is my granddaughter. She's all the family I have."

As quickly as her anger had come, it turned to tears.

Now what was I going to do?

"I'm sorry, Mrs. Kenwood. Truly, I'm sorry for your losses. I shouldn't have come today." I turned to leave.

She raised her head and again gestured for me to sit down.

"Excuse my emotion, young lady. It's not becoming."

"Can I sit over there by you?" I startled myself and her with the question.

"Yes, I suppose so. Make yourself comfortable." She pushed her things aside, and I sat down next to her.

"I was angry earlier — at myself mostly — for not finding this out sooner," I explained as she daintily blew her nose. "I was mad because I'm the one who has to tell Destiny, and how on earth will I ever do it? What shattering news! She was just beginning to get used to the idea of having a grandmother, of having a piece of her past and her family back."

116

"I'm still her grandmother," she said haughtily.

"Of course you are," I reassured her. "But somewhere out there, there's another mother and father. I'm not sure how much more of this she can take. Or I can take, for that matter."

"Perhaps you shouldn't tell her just now."

"Oh no!" I shook my head vehemently. "I care for her too much to do that. She's the best friend I've ever had. Plus, she'd kill me if she knew I wasn't truthful with her."

"She always was quite stubborn, so I suppose you're right."

"I am right," I said glumly.

"It wasn't fair," Mrs. Kenwood said.

"It certainly wasn't," I agreed, unable to figure out how I was going to tell Destiny the full extent of her life's injustices.

"Peter and Barbara were so in love. It wasn't fair they couldn't have children. Barbara was crushed when they found out. And Peter, well my Peter tried to hide it, but you could see the disappointment in his eyes every time he saw a child. Then came the news from the church that a baby girl was available, and you should have seen the two of them. They were positively giddy. No two people could have loved a child more than they loved Destiny."

"How old was she when they got her?"

"A little over a week old. When I held her, I thought she'd melt in my arms." Happiness radiated in the older woman's eyes as she remembered that moment.

"Who handled the adoption?"

"St. Peter's, of course. They took care of her both times."

"Do you know anything about the mother — or father — who gave her up?"

Her eyes turned cold in an instant.

"No, I don't, and what does it matter? After all these years, what does it matter? How can it rightly compare to the years of love we gave that child? She was ours! Make no mistake of that!" she snapped.

Although my timing may have been bad, my intention wasn't.

"Probably it doesn't matter, Mrs. Kenwood," I said gently. "I hope it doesn't. But Destiny has to be the one to decide. I'm only the messenger, and I promised to get her as much information about her past as I could. I hope you understand."

She started to cry again, tears that fell slowly.

"It wasn't fair. I was afraid to tell you because I thought she wouldn't care about us, that all she'd want was her real family.

It's important that she knows how special she was to us."

"She does know," I reassured her, hoping to stop the tears. "She wouldn't trade the other night for the world."

"It was a splendid evening, wasn't it?" She smiled weakly.

"It was," I agreed.

The clock chimed, and I jumped from my seat when I saw what time it was.

"I have to be going now."

"So soon?"

"I'm afraid so. I have a call to make, and then I've got to catch Destiny as soon as she gets home from work."

"Be gentle with her," she ordered.

"I will. And I'm sorry for bursting in on you like that. Sometimes my temper gets the best of me."

"It's refreshing to meet one as forthright as you, Kristin, even if it can be disturbing."

"Thanks." There was a compliment in there somewhere.

"Drive carefully."

"I will."

"Call me soon. I'd like to have you girls over for dinner again sometime... if you'll still come."

"We will," I promised for both of us, hoping I'd be able to make good on the promise.

• • •

The second I got home, before I could even take off my coat, I called Benjamin Greaves.

Fortunately, most of the fight was gone from me by the time he came to the phone.

"Hello, Kristin."

"Hi. Listen, I have to ask you something. And I need the truth. No bullshit, okay?"

"You don't waste words, do you? What can I do for you?"

"Did you know Destiny was adopted?" I tried to sound stern and accusing but came off sounding weak and petulant.

His hearty laughter just about damaged my eardrum.

"That's a good one, Kristin. I enjoy your sense of humor."

"I'm serious."

"Of course I knew she was adopted. I adopted her now, didn't I?" He laughed again.

I couldn't tell if he was toying with me, or if he really didn't

118

know. Gamely, I plunged forward.

"Not by you." I hesitated. "Did you know the Kenwoods adopted her, that Barbara and Peter weren't Destiny's natural parents?"

There was no laughter this time.

"That's a sick joke," he said fiercely.

"I'm not joking. One of Barbara's friends, a Lydia Barton, let it slip when I was interviewing her, and then Marie Kenwood confirmed it an hour ago. The Kenwoods adopted her when she was a week old."

"Why wasn't I told?" he shouted.

"I don't know. Mrs. Kenwood assumed you knew, and she assumed you told me, which of course, you didn't."

"I never knew!" The anguish in his voice was now equal to the anger. "Good Lord, what will I tell Liz? This will kill her. She's had enough trouble trying to contend with Barbara Kenwood's image and now this. It will devastate her." He sounded more like her husband than her ex-husband.

"No offense, but my main concern right now is Destiny."

"Of course. Of course. I can't even think about what this will mean to her. She's seemed so peaceful lately, especially after she met her grandmother. Or the woman she thought was her grandmother. I can't even think of it—another mother. My God, another father!"

"Please don't say anything to Destiny. I'm going to try to call her as soon as we're done here, but in case I can't reach her, please wait to talk to her."

"You're not honestly thinking of telling her now, are you?"

Suddenly, I was the target of his anger.

"I am."

"Don't!" His tone was menacing.

"I have to."

"You can't! Haven't you done enough?"

"No," I said in a quiet, angry voice. "There will be no more secrets! There's no point in them."

"I hope someday you can forgive yourself for what you're about to do to my daughter," he retorted.

And then there was a dial tone.

119

17

I didn't waste a second. My paranoia had reached new heights. I was afraid that in his angry state, Benjamin Greaves would call Destiny and then whisk her off to some faraway land, safely out of my reach.

I was never more grateful to hear someone's voice than I was when Destiny said "Hello."

"Destiny, thank God you're home!"

"What's wrong, Kris, you sound terrible."

"I have to talk to you. Can I come over?"

"Sure, come right now if you want."

"I'm on my way."

"Are you sure you can drive? You sound really upset."

"I'm fine. I'll see you in a few minutes."

• • •

With every ounce of energy I had, I concentrated on my driving. I knew Destiny thought something was wrong with me. I knew she'd be preparing herself to comfort me. I knew her misunderstanding would make it all the more difficult for me to tell her what I needed to, but I couldn't have said anything more on the phone.

I was still reeling from my whirlwind afternoon when I burst through her door and perched myself on the edge of the couch.

"I've got some bad news —"

"What is it?" she interrupted me, her concern apparent.

"Please, Destiny, this is hard enough for me. Let me just spit it out," I said, my voice cracking with emotion. "Today, I found out you're adopted."

She started to smile, and she looked like she was going to interrupt me again.

I put up a hand to silence her.

"Not by your parents, Liz and Benjamin Greaves. By the Kenwoods. They weren't your natural parents. They adopted you when you were a week old."

In her eyes, I read shock, disbelief, and finally anger.

"Very funny, Kris!"

"I'm not joking," I said wearily. "Everyone seems to think I have a warped sense of humor today. I don't. I'm dead serious. Lydia Barton let it slip this afternoon. I've been to your grandma's, and she confirmed it. I'm sorry."

"No, no, no, no." She started sobbing.

I didn't know what to do, how to comfort her. I wanted to touch her, to hold her, but I wasn't sure how to approach her. The louder she cried, the more awkward I felt. As her breathing became faster, I started to panic. Unable to do more, I finally decided to sit down next to her. When I reached over to pat her leg, she grabbed me, almost frantically, and hugged me.

It was almost an hour before she stopped crying and was able to breathe normally again. The whole time, I held her, and the physical touch felt good. I tried to will my strength into her body. I lightly stroked her hair. I told her everything would be okay, though I didn't have the faintest idea if it really would be. Mostly, I listened to her grief filling the room and tried not to drown in it.

"Tell me exactly what they told you," she commanded when at last she raised her head to look at me.

Still holding her hand, I told her all about my afternoon.

"I can't believe my father never knew!"

"Unless he's the world's greatest liar, he never knew. He was as shocked as I was."

"He's a terrible liar."

"Then he never knew."

"I can't believe I sat at that woman's house for three hours and she let me believe I was her granddaughter."

"You were, Destiny. You are. Nothing changes the years you two spent together."

"Still, I would have appreciated hearing this little tidbit a few days sooner."

"She was afraid of losing you."

"For good reason. She has lost me."

I went along with her anger, knowing she didn't mean it but wanting to show I supported her.

"Maybe it is best you don't see her again. You've been through a lot lately. A break would do you good."

"I did enjoy myself the other night."

"Yeah, but it's too stressful."

"Actually, it was the most healing thing I've ever done."

"She'd probably be a burden on you anyway."

"Not at all. I thought she was independent and charming."

"So did I. Plus she invited us over for dinner again." I smiled at her slyly.

She hit me with a pillow.

"Kris, you really are a terror!"

"I know."

"My mother will die when she hears this. She's always been very concerned with what other people think, and this won't set well with her. She's constantly flaunting other people's accomplishments in front of me, as if life were some sort of race and I'm not running fast enough. Appearances mean a lot to her. This is not going to look good. She'll die!"

"Your dad said the same thing. Except his words were 'This will kill her.'"

"He's right. Maybe I should call her, and hell, maybe I should call him, too."

"And say what?"

"I don't know!" She threw up her hands in frustration. "I'm sorry I'm not your real daughter. I'm sorry I found my real family and then discovered they weren't my real family. Or how about this: I'm sorry I was ever born."

"Oh, c'mon. You know you're not. You know they're not. You know Marie Kenwood's not. For that matter, you better know I'm not sorry you were born."

"Thanks." Destiny winked at me, her self-pity instantly gone. "By the way, I'm a free woman," she said flippantly, hiding the pain I knew she must feel. "Last Saturday, I told Michelle I don't want to date anymore. I'm sure she's already spread the news, but I wanted you to hear it from me."

"She did tell me. Are you okay?"

"I'm getting by. I'm lonely, but I feel better. The kind of relationships I've had in the past aren't enough for me now. Remember when you first told me about the incest, when you said all you wanted was a safe place to sleep?"

I nodded.

"After you told me that, I couldn't stop thinking about what you said. I think I've been looking for the same thing all these years. I'm embarrassed to tell you how many women's beds I've been in and left, looking for that place and never finding it. I mean think about my life, Kris, not my life now, but my life as a four-year-old. One night, I'm having a great time at my grandma's, the next morning I wake up and she tells me my parents are dead. Gone forever and all I did was close my eyes. So now, I think I lure all these women into bed, because on some level, I need the comfort of always having someone lying next to me, just in case there's another horrible night."

"But there will never again be one that bad, Destiny. Never!"

"I know that, but the child in me still looks for comfort."

"But the adult in you realizes you barely know the woman you just had sex with, and you feel awkward staying and being intimate with a stranger, so you leave in the middle of the night, right?"

Destiny just looked at me, her mouth wide open.

"You're scary sometimes, Kris."

"What? Am I right? Is that how you feel?"

"I would never have used those words to describe it, but yes, that's exactly how I feel. It's eerie how much you know."

She paused to look at me intently, almost as if she were seeing me for the first time.

"Anyway, I want more. But I also know I'm nowhere near ready for more. It wasn't fair to drag Michelle through all this. I want to be more clear before I get involved with anyone. Who knows, maybe it'll even be Michelle when I'm ready."

"I doubt it."

"Why?"

"What you found attractive in her a month ago, you no longer find attractive as you open yourself up and ask for more commitment, more trust. Michelle isn't capable of what you need."

"Sometimes, Kris, you're brutally honest."

"Is that good or bad?"

"When I'm ready to hear it, it's good."

"And the rest of the time?"

124

"It's a damn irritating habit."

We both laughed and then were silent, lost in thought. When at last I looked over at her, I caught her openly staring at me.

"Hey, Kris."

"Hey what?"

"Let's have sex."

I couldn't tell if she was serious.

"Are you kidding me?"

"What kind of an answer is that? No woman's ever said that to my proposal."

"I'm serious, Destiny. Are you kidding?"

"Only halfway. You must know I have a crush on you."

"I was beginning to suspect," I managed to say in a voice that was conspicuously deep, then I quickly coughed.

"I've had a crush on you since the day I met you, and the more time I spend with you, the worse it gets. Will you stay the night with me?" Her tone was deliberately light, but I could see the seriousness in her eyes.

My heart was racing.

She was leaning back in the folds of the couch, half sitting, half lying down. I saw the light from the fire that caught the color in her hair. I saw her slender hands, clasped in front of her in a relaxed fashion. I saw the curve of her neck and the curve of her breasts behind her cotton shirt.

I saw all of these parts of her that I'd been afraid to notice before.

"I'll probably regret this the rest of my life," I coughed again, "but I need a friend now far more than I need a lover, and so do you, Destiny."

She dismissed my seriousness with a sweep of her hand.

"And furthermore," I swallowed hard, "I know that if we made love, I'd never let go. How could I ever make love with you and not fall in love?"

Her eyes filled up with tears.

"That's the nicest thing anyone's ever said to me."

"It's true." I was having trouble breathing.

"For what it's worth, Kris, I don't think I could leave you in the middle of the night."

"I should hope not. I'd shoot you when I caught up with you the next day."

Mercifully, my humor broke the sexual tension.

"No sex?" she tried one more time.

I shook my head.

"Damn. Then how about a movie? I could use a little escapism right about now."

"I'd be happy to take you to the movies."

"I'll get my coat."

"Great."

As we were leaving the house, I held the door open for her.

"In the excitement of the day, I forgot to tell you the good news, that you were a budding lesbian at the age of four."

She laughed heartily.

"You're making this up to cheer me up."

"I'm not, I swear it. You had a best friend who lived next door, Lydia Barton's daughter. Her name was Janine, but you called her honey."

She hit me with her coat.

"I knew you were lying."

"Okay, seriously, you called her Nene. That was your very first word."

"My girlfriend's name was the first word out of my mouth?"

"It was."

"That figures. I always was advanced," she said obviously impressed by her early tastes. "Was she cute?"

"When she was little, she was adorable. Her mother has a ton of photos of her on display in the living room. Now, I'd say she's average-looking," I perhaps understated.

"What's she up to these days?"

"Funny you should ask. Get this — she lives in San Francisco with her 'best friend' who's an electrician."

"Hot damn! Is it presumptuous of me to stereotype?"

"Not at all. She's a lesbian if I ever saw one."

"How funny."

"You don't remember her at all?"

"When you said her name, I had a flash of memory, but it went away before I could catch it."

"Maybe more will come back to you later."

"You're sure she's only average-looking now?"

"Maybe a fraction above average," I conceded. "But she seems to be a married woman."

"No matter. Let's go visit her, Kris. Let's skip the movie and fly to San Francisco."

"Oh sure!"

"Let's do it!" She jumped up and down. "You're the boss. Close the office for a few days. Let's go meet Janine."

"You're serious?"

The twinkle in her eye gave her away.

"Only halfway. But it would be an adventure, wouldn't it?"

"Every moment with you is an adventure, Destiny."

• • •

We didn't go to San Francisco. We went to a movie that wasn't meant to be a comedy and laughed our heads off. We ate dinner at the theater — nachos and popcorn.

I went home alone.

When I got back to my apartment, I started cleaning it. Three hours later, I still wasn't done. It wasn't so much the cleaning that took time. It was the picking things up. I hauled piles and piles of stuff from the living room into the bedroom. And from the bedroom into the bathroom. And from every room into the kitchen. I wore myself out before I ever turned the vacuum on, which was probably just as well given that it was way past midnight.

On impulse, when I was straightening up the phone cord, I called Destiny.

"Hello." Thankfully, her voice didn't sound groggy.

"Hi, it's me. What are you doing?"

"Actually, I was getting ready for bed. What's up?"

"Not much. I just wanted to see if you were okay."

"I'm okay. Are you okay?"

"Of course I am. I had a very eventful day, a wonderful evening with a good friend, and I cleaned my apartment."

"You cleaned your apartment tonight?"

"Yep."

"You cleaned your apartment instead of having sex with me?" Her voice was full of mock outrage.

"Well, I never thought of it in those terms, but now that you mention it, yes."

"I'm insulted."

"Don't be. My apartment has gotten quite dirty while I've given you and your case my sole attention."

"That's better." We both laughed. "Did you call because you had one of those dreams, Kris?" she asked me quite seriously.

"No, not at all. I haven't even tried to sleep. I just called to see how you were."

"That's nice of you, but really, I'm fine."

"Has it sunk in yet that you have three mothers?"

"To tell you the truth, I've been trying not to think about it. When I got home, I took a nice long bath and I've been reading."

"Good, I just wanted to make sure you're okay."

"I'm fine, Kris. Really, I am. But if you're still concerned, you could come over here and check up on me."

"Very funny," I said, smiling despite myself.

"I'm serious," she said laughing.

"Oh, sure."

"It was a crazy day today, wasn't it?"

"It certainly was."

"Hey, Kris —"

"Hey what?"

"You wouldn't be too terribly disappointed if we quit looking for any more members of my family, would you?"

"Not at all," I said, which wasn't really true.

"I'm not sure I can take much more of this."

"That's okay. You've been through a lot already."

"You've helped me tremendously, you know."

"I know."

"You're sure you're not disappointed?"

"Of course not!" I lied ineffectively.

"You sound disappointed."

"Even if we're done looking for people, can we still be friends?" I asked tentatively.

"Of course, we can! Is that what you're worried about?"

"A little."

"Don't be. It's been a long time since I met anyone I liked as much as you, Kristin Ashe. We've only just begun."

"Good."

"And I may keep going with the search, but I'm not sure. I need a couple of days to think about it."

"Take all the time you need. I could use a break myself."

"I will. And don't forget to call me if you want to talk in the middle of the night... and not just about me."

"I will," I said grinning. On that note, we said our good-byes.

• • •

As I lay in bed that night, naked and alone, I thought about all the reasons I wanted to make love with Destiny, and there were many. Then I thought about all the reasons why I hadn't, and there were even more.

Making love with the most beautiful, dynamic woman in Denver would have been so easy... and so incredibly exciting. In my thoughts, we did make love, and it was wonderful. Full of love and life and laughter. That was the fantasy.

The reality was that I'd already made love with the most beautiful, dynamic woman in Denver.

Her name was Gallagher, and she was gone. From my life and almost completely from my heart.

On our first date, Gallagher had taught me to dance. Over my strong protestations, she took me out onto the dance floor, held me tight, and taught me how to feel the music, which was really just a process of learning to unfeel the fear. On that night, I discovered the sensuous art of dance and felt the beginning twinges of intimacy. I wanted, for the first time in my life, to be touched. To be physically comforted. Gallagher held me in her powerful arms and for a time, my mind was quiet.

It didn't last long.

Over time, my body closed down. I worked and worked to allow it to stay open, but I couldn't. I avoided making love, afraid to tell her that I couldn't stand to be touched.

I immersed myself in work, like an alcoholic in drink. I was afraid my business was failing. Except it wasn't. Sales went up and up. Costs went down and down. The employees were happy. The clients were happy. Only I was dissatisfied.

And then one day, she left.

That night, I had wanted to make love with Destiny.

But I knew I wasn't ready.

By nature, I was a loner. Making love brought me out of my own cold world into a magical one of warm, loving touch. Eventually, though, my instincts, honed from years of survival, destroyed the magic, and I recoiled at a lover's touch.

I knew this.

Over and over again, I'd tried to recreate the past. I'd tried to teach myself the basic lessons of love and touch. But either I wasn't a very good teacher, or I wasn't a very good learner. In any case, I wasn't a very good lover.

Distance always prevailed.

18

Several days passed before I talked to Destiny again. In those days, my life returned to normal. I concentrated on work when I was at work. I rode my bike all over Denver. I even managed to squeeze in a trip to the mountains. All was peaceful.

When I did have occasion to call, it was because I was honoring my word. On Wednesday night, I went to bed as usual but awoke with a start from the most horrifying dream.

Someone is trying to do sexual things with me. Puts his hands between my legs. Puts his penis between my legs from behind.

I hear Ann and Gail in the other room talking about him. They don't want to sleep with him anymore.

I somehow hide from him. Run upstairs to tell my mom. Usually she sleeps with him. I am going to tell her I am too old to be sleeping with him.

I am going to tell her he doesn't know what he is doing — she should talk to him.

Before I can say anything, she looks at me like "What now? I can't handle one more thing."

Slowly, I close her bedroom door.

I hide from the man, hoping he'll go to Ann and Gail's room.

• • •

Still shaking from the dream, I sat up and used the sheets to wipe the sweat from my body.

When my breathing returned to normal, I called Destiny. After what seemed like a hundred rings, she answered.

"Kris, is that you?"

"How'd you know it was me?" I lamely attempted humor.

"Are you okay?"

"No." I answered the question honestly for, perhaps, the first time in my life.

"Did you dream?"

"Yes," I said, my voice shaking, my body still trembling.

"Can you talk to me about it?"

"No," I mumbled.

"Could you try, Kris? It might make it easier," she said in a gentle voice.

"I can't. I'll cry."

"Crying's okay. Remember? You're the one who helped me learn to cry again."

Slowly, haltingly, I told her about the dream. Several times she had to ask me to repeat sentences because my crying made the words indistinguishable.

"It's okay. It's okay," she repeated soothingly as I struggled to regain control.

"What am I going to do?" I asked, the pain clear in the timbre of my voice.

"Do you want me to come over? I could be there in ten minutes, fifteen tops. I'll get dressed while we talk on the phone."

"No, that's not what I meant. I'm okay for now, but what am I going to do tomorrow, Destiny? What am I going to do about the fact that I have a mother who emotionally abused me and a father who..." my voice broke again, "... who sexually abused me?"

"I don't know. I wish there was an answer."

"When, for God's sake, will it ever stop hurting?" I asked angrily. "When?"

"You know, Kris, it's okay for it to hurt. For years, I blocked out the pain and blocked out a hell of a lot of other feelings, too. I tried to protect myself by forgetting everything, but now I see that actually prevented me from healing. Finally, I'm starting to allow myself to feel the loss, thanks to you, and as much as it hurts, and as weird as this sounds, it's great!"

"Then you think this is good that I'm dreaming, as awful as it is, because it's healing?"

"Exactly. It's another sign of how you're not pretending anymore, how you're grieving instead. It's an incredibly big step."

"But it feels so unsettling."

"Of course it does. You've never done it before. You've lived in your mind and closed down your heart and your body. But you're changing. If you think about it, calling me may be one of the most healing things you've done. When you have these dreams, don't you usually try to ignore them, and hope they'll go away?"

"Yes," I agreed tentatively.

"Even though they hurt like hell and scare you to death, don't you usually pretend they don't?"

"Of course I do! I don't want them to have that kind of power over me, that suffocating control."

"Of course you don't, but the fact is, Kris, they do have that power. They do hurt and they do scare you. But tonight, instead of taking away their power by pretending, you called me up and talked to me, right?"

"I guess."

"You see then, you're healing!"

"But didn't it bug you that I woke you up?"

"Not at all!"

"Didn't it disgust you to hear about the things I dreamed?"

"What your father did to you disgusts me. What you dreamed doesn't. I know you feel a lot of shame, but you don't need to. You were a helpless little kid. You no more caused the incest than I caused my parents' death, but I know that's hard for you to believe. To this day, I have trouble believing I was blameless."

"But isn't it horrible that I wanted him to attack Ann and Gail. How could I be so awful to wish that on anyone?"

"You were trying to survive. The best way a child could."

"God, isn't it frightening?"

"Which part?"

"Parents literally own children. They can treat them any way they please, and it's all perfectly legal. Unless they scald them to death in the bathtub or beat them until they have head injuries or rape them so obviously that no adults can turn their heads, no one notices. Parents completely control what their children are taught and who they become. If they please, they give them food. If not, they don't. If they want, they give them medical care. If not, they die.

"Think of it, Destiny, it's frightening. They control whether we live or die. And if they are kind enough to let us live, they control our quality of life. Worse, they set the standards. Until we're well into our adult years, we don't even realize that not everyone's family was like ours. That maybe we were deprived. That maybe they were depraved.

"And all the while, as children, we are like some kind of live receptacles for guilt and shame. We store it in our little bodies, we guard it with our lives, as if we were waiting for someone to retrieve it, but they never do. And then, when we become adults, we have so much trouble emptying it because we've learned to guard it so well."

We were both quiet for a moment, then Destiny spoke.

"Let's make a pact. Let's keep working together to empty it. I'll support you and you can support me, okay?"

"Sounds like friendship to me," I joked because I was taken aback by the intimacy of her proposal.

"It is. Does that scare you?"

"Yes," was all I could say. I didn't want to start crying again.

"But you could easily support me, right? You've been doing a great job of supporting me since we met."

"Oh, yeah, no problem. I don't mind supporting you at all."

"But it's hard for you to let me support you, right?"

"A little," I understated the obvious.

"It's hard for you to receive, isn't it? You know how to give, but you can't receive."

"Yes," I whispered "Funny you should say that. Gallagher said almost that exact same thing to me, right before she left." I cleared my throat. "One night we were making love and I started to make love to her, but she stopped me. She said, 'Let me make love to you, Kris. Just this once, please receive. It's been so long.' And it had been. I never was very good at receiving." I started to cry softly.

"You must miss Gallagher a lot."

"I do," I wailed.

"Michelle told me you two were quite a couple."

"We were." I cried even harder.

"She also told me you never talked about the break-up, that you acted like it was no big deal."

"It was a huge deal," I said defensively. "But Michelle never would have understood. What was the point in talking to her?"

"Did you talk to anyone?"

"Ann. A little. Not much."

"What happened? Can you talk about it now?"

"She loved me too much, Destiny, and it scared me. I couldn't

134

take it anymore. I could never let her see how much I loved her. Late at night, so many nights, after she'd fallen asleep, I'd light a candle and watch her sleep. I'd touch her hair softly and I'd tell her how much I loved her. Only then could I really love her with all my heart. That was the only time I felt completely safe expressing my love — when no one else could see it, not even her."

"You were afraid to love her," Destiny said, her voice barely above a whisper.

"I was afraid of everything. I still am."

"No wonder you had trouble making love."

"No kidding! Most of the time when we made love, my body was there, but I couldn't quiet my brain. These horrible, incomplete thoughts would race in and out as I struggled to concentrate on the sex. And then, on the rare occasions when we made love and I wasn't scared, by the time we really connected, the closeness terrified me. Invariably, the day after we made love, we'd get into this huge fight. I never could be close to her for very long. I tried and tried, but I couldn't do it."

Destiny didn't say anything.

"I miss her the most in the middle of the night. She adored me. No one had ever adored me before. She'd laugh at all my jokes, even if they were dumb, and I'd laugh at hers. Sometimes, we'd stay awake for hours, laughing at the silliest things. It was like the slumber parties I used to go to when I was a kid, except better, because we were both naked, and it was just the two of us. My God, she was my best friend." I couldn't seem to stop talking.

"She sounds wonderful."

"Not a day goes by that I don't wonder what happened to us. I really thought she was my life partner. Do you believe in life partners, Destiny?"

"I'm not sure. I don't think I've met mine yet. Well, maybe I did. Maybe Janine, my first love, was a candidate, but you'd know more about that than I would," she kidded.

"Very funny. You told me you couldn't even remember her."

"I can't, but I'll bet I trusted her, don't you think?"

"I'm sure you did."

"It's too bad I had to lose Janine, too. And my grandma."

"It is," I agreed.

"I think I'd like to see my grandma again. Do you think she'll agree to see me, even though I'm not her real granddaughter?"

"Of course, she will! She'd be thrilled to see you again! She wants to have us over for dinner. Do you want me to call her and set something up?"

"No, thanks for offering, but I think I can do it this time. Will you come with me again?"

"You bet!"

"Even if I invite Lydia Barton?"

"Sure, but are you you ready for all that?"

"I think so, Kris. I've been doing a lot of thinking lately, preparing myself really. Speaking of which, if it wouldn't be too much, I'd like to keep looking for the rest of my family. Will you help me find my mother — and father, if possible?"

"Of course I'll help you."

"Everybody thinks I'm crazy, that I should stop, but I'm not done yet. My father called to lecture me about what all this has done to my mother. For God's sake, you'd think they were still married, the way he acts. Then my mother called to ask me what my problem was, weren't she and my father good enough?"

"What did you tell her?"

"I told her I need to take care of myself. I told her what I'm doing is hard and that while I didn't expect her support, I didn't deserve her criticism either. I asked her not to call me anymore. I told her I'd come see her and explain things to her as soon as I possibly could. In the meantime, I need space."

"Whew! What did she say to all that?"

"She said I never had appreciated all the things she and my father gave me. At which point, I kind of yelled back that I'd appreciated them every single damn minute of my life because I lived in constant fear of losing them. She told me I didn't even wear the gown she chose for the debutante ball. I informed her I never wanted to be a debutante in the first place, that it wasn't me, but that I'd gone through with it to please her. Can you believe this woman, Kris? Ten years later, she's still mad that I didn't wear the dress she liked. I went to the goddamn ball. All these things I did for her all my life, because on some level, I was afraid that if I didn't do them, she wouldn't let me stay. But they were never enough. Anyway, I kind of lost my temper and she hung up in the middle of me screaming at her."

"Did you call her back?"

"Not hardly. I've needed the break from her. I'm sorry it had to come to this, but at the same time, I'm relieved. Some days, when I'm really discouraged, I think she'll never accept me for who I am. To this day, she still sends me money in the mail. Every month, I get an envelope with cash in it. She used to send me checks, but years ago, I told her to stop, so now she sends the money anonymously, and we both pretend that she doesn't do it. The only thing I can do to keep my sanity is donate it to the most radical lesbian cause I can find. She'd have a heart attack if she knew about the kinds of donations I've made in her name."

"Good for you."

"It's funny — I've done so many things other people would call courageous, and yet I can't do the simplest thing in the world — tell my mother what's in my heart," she said with disgust.

"Don't be so hard on yourself, Destiny. It may seem simple but it's never easy."

"My work is really ironic, too. That's part of what I've been thinking about lately. I think I'm good at what I do because of my mother. In dealing with her, I learned to be a supreme negotiator. I've lived my whole life working the system, compromising, giving her what she wanted while trying to get some things I needed. There's nothing courageous in that. I've worked and worked to save the world when I couldn't even save myself."

"C'mon, you've done a lot of people a lot of good."

"I know that. I've always known that. But it's not enough anymore to take care of other people when I can't take care of myself. That's why I've decided to take a leave of absence from my work."

"You're kidding!"

"I'm not. I've never been more serious. The world needs so much saving, Kris. It can do without me for a month, or even a year."

"Would you take a whole year off?"

"Maybe. I'm committed to taking as much time as I need."

"I'm shocked! You *are* your work, Destiny!"

"No, I'm not," she said with a heavy sigh. "Until recently, I thought I was, but I'm not. My work is a part of me, but it's not all of me. There are other parts of me, too, most of which I've let die because I was so busy with my work. Now I'm finally doing something just for me. You should join me — take a month off. We could travel, see the world, find ourselves."

"Don't tempt me."

"You're not ready to let go of your work, though, are you?" she asked seriously.

"No, I'm not. It protects me," I said simply.

"Oh well, it was just a thought."

We chatted for a few more minutes. I thanked her for talking to me in the dark hours of the night. She thanked me for calling her. Before we hung up, I asked her to call her father to get the names of the people in the church who had handled her adoption to the Greaves.

As I straightened the sheets on my bed, I thought how lucky I was to have a friend like Destiny.

Maybe I was changing, I thought as I fell asleep. Just maybe.

Dawn had barely broken when I screamed myself awake.

Destiny and I are visiting my family. After some horrible fight, I decide to leave. I tell Ann and Gail I'm leaving. I talk to them separately. I yell at them, trying to get them to understand me. Over and over, I scream, "I haven't betrayed you! I haven't betrayed you!"

This time, I didn't call anyone, and I didn't bother trying to get back to sleep. I got up and went to work.

CHAPTER

19

Given my early arrival at work, I was the only one there for several hours. When Ann came in at her usual time of 9 a.m., she popped into my office before she started working.

"So, how are things going with Destiny?"

"Have a seat," I offered after she helped herself to my couch. "So far I've found three mothers."

"No!"

"Really."

I straightened the work on my desk into piles so I wouldn't lose track of what I'd been doing. Then I opened the bottom drawer of my desk, kicked back in my chair, and propped my feet on the drawer. I proceeded to explain Destiny's complicated family tree to Ann. In the end, she shook her head in disbelief.

"I can't believe that! How awful!"

"Neither can I, except I keep finding it out one little piece at a time, so it's easier to absorb."

"How's Michelle reacting to all of this?"

"Funny you should ask...."

"What? I suppose Michelle is Destiny's long-lost sister."

I laughed.

"No, nothing that sensational. Destiny broke up with her last week."

"Huh. How's Michelle handling it?"

"Superbly, as always. She's chasing after some veterinarian. She's contemplating taking her cats in for vaccinations they don't need. I told her it might not be so good for their health, but I doubt she listened to me."

"Boy, she doesn't waste any time, does she?"

"Nope. Enough about her, though. I wanted to talk about you and me... and about us." I sat up in my chair, closed the desk drawer, took a paper clip from the top of my desk and started fiddling with it.

"Okay...." Ann said, looking a little uncomfortable.

"I've been dreaming some more..." I started slowly, "... about the incest."

"And you're sure it's Dad?"

"Positive."

She looked stricken. I felt stricken. I put the paper clip down and started doodling on my desk pad. I drew kites, which were the only thing I ever sketched, and used different colored pens to fill them in.

"It's hard to believe, isn't it?"

"Impossible," I said wearily. "Have you had any memories of it?" I asked hopefully.

At first, she didn't reply.

"No. No, I haven't. But it feels like something happened. Ever since you asked me if I thought he molested us, I can't stop feeling like he probably did. Andrea, my therapist, thinks maybe it's time she and I started working on him in our sessions. But just the thought of it makes my stomach hurt. What are we going to do, Kris?"

"I don't know."

"Do you think you'll confront Dad?"

"Oh, God, no!" A chill ran up my spine at the very thought. "I'm not ready for that yet."

"Good," she said, much relieved, for she knew that my confrontation would result in hers as well.

"It's funny, Ann, but I don't think that's the most pressing thing. Most of the work has to be done inside me. Before I can confront him, I have to first confront my own feelings.

"You know, I've run all over the city for Destiny, gathering memories and facing people, and I've seen that what I've done for her has helped. But most of what's changed Destiny is Destiny. The day she hired me, she allowed herself to start feeling again — things she'd blocked twenty-five years ago and even a month ago. I want to start feeling again, too, instead of blocking everything, then maybe I'll be ready to face Dad."

"You already have started feeling, Kris. We're talking about it, aren't we?"

"We are... and this will probably shock you, but I'm going to take some time off work, time to stop running from it."

"You can't be serious!"

"I am," I said quietly, taking my glasses off to wipe the sweat off my eyebrows. "God, it's hot in here, maybe we should turn down the heat."

"The heat's not on."

"Huh, well, I'm going to take a few days off, maybe a month."

"You never take time off, especially not since Gallagher left."

"Then it's about time I did, right?"

"I don't know," she replied, the shock still evident on her face. "I can't picture you not working. You always work."

"Don't worry," I assured her, "I don't have any firm plans yet. It's just a thought. I'll give you plenty of notice if I decide to do it."

"You've gone off the deep-end," Ann said, with more affection than judgment.

"I know," I laughed. "It's great, isn't it?"

● ● ●

That night, Destiny and I went to a photography exhibit at the Denver Art Museum. We both pretended to know more about art than we did. We laughed a lot and saw very little. Almost as an afterthought, as she was getting out of the car at her house, she gave me the name of Sister Margaret Kincaid — the nun who had introduced her to the Greaves family.

I fell asleep that night thinking of what it must have been like to take a four-year-old Destiny from her grandmother's arms. And I dreamed.

I am kissing my father, long and slow on the lips. We are standing up, in the basement by the washer and dryer. I am older, maybe even my own age.

He's telling me how attractive I am. I am putting up with it to get information, to see if he'll really do it, to be able to have proof. It's absolutely revolting.

I got up and took a long, hot bath. I hopped back into bed and for a change, instantly fell into a deep sleep.

I didn't wake up until the alarm went off.

Maybe I was beginning to heal from the wounds of misplaced

touch and broken trust. Slowly but surely, maybe I was.

• • •

As soon as I arrived at work, I made a few simple, if deceitful, calls to the Archdiocese of Denver and easily located Sister Margaret Kincaid. She was working as a secretary in one of the parish's elementary schools.

In the afternoon, I met her at the school, right before the last bell rang.

We talked in her cramped, windowless office. I sat on the other side of her cluttered desk and tried not to look at her. Her red-orange hair bothered me, as did the black-framed glasses with half-inch-thick lenses that rested in stark contrast to her pale complexion.

I began by explaining why I was there. I told her I wanted to find out more about the Kenwoods, that I was doing this as a favor to the daughter they left behind when they died. Between pursed lips, she curtly told me she knew who Destiny Greaves was, that she read the papers and watched the evening news.

In a quiet voice, she answered my questions with speed and precision.

"How well did you know the Kenwoods?"

"I knew of them. They'd been active in our parish for several years."

"Can you tell me what they were like?"

"I believe they were good people. They attended church every Sunday."

"When did you first meet Destiny?"

"The day after her parents died. Father O'Malley suggested I visit the grandmother and the child — to offer the church's condolences. He set up the appointment."

"Were you the one who decided where she'd spend the rest of her life?"

"I decided nothing. I met with the grandmother and she asked for the church's assistance. We found a suitable family for the child."

"In the form of Benjamin and Liz Greaves?"

"Yes."

"What made them suitable?" I finally looked directly at her. "How were they matched up with Destiny?"

"They were available and they agreed to adopt her."

142

"That's it? Nothing more?"

"They were screened, of course. Once the couple came forward, there was procedure to be followed. Father O'Malley interviewed the father and mother several times. I accompanied him to their house for these visits."

"Were there any other couples available, other than the Greaves, who wanted to adopt Destiny?"

"Not that I recall."

"Did you ever see Destiny again after that first visit?"

"Of course. I made several follow-up visits to the Greaves' home. It was my duty to assist the family in making a smooth transition."

Smooth transition, ha, I wanted to yell. Ripping a child away from everyone and everything she knew couldn't possibly have been smoothed over by a couple of afternoon socials. I checked my temper before I spoke.

"At those visits, how did Destiny seem to you?"

For the briefest moment, the Sister looked embarrassed.

"I really couldn't say. She rarely joined in on our visits, so I didn't see much of her. She was a very independent child."

Try sad and alone and four-years-old, not independent, I wanted to shout at this woman who probably could not hear.

"You went on these visits to help Destiny adjust to the Greaves family, yet you never saw her?"

Talk about saved by the bell. It rang and the older woman never had a chance to answer that question.

"I must be going now, Miss Ashe. Thank you for stopping by." She stood up from behind her desk and escorted me into the hall and back to the building's main entrance.

"Just a minute, Sister Margaret. I have one more question...."

Behind me, children were shuffling papers and closing books, readying themselves to bolt out into the hallways.

"Can you tell me the name of the Sister who handled Destiny's first adoption — when the Kenwoods adopted her as an infant?"

Her face lost what little color it had.

Nervously, she glanced around to see if anyone was near.

"I don't know what you're talking about," she stammered.

"Look," I said deepening my voice to its lowest octave, "I know everything. The grandmother told me Destiny was adopted and she also told me St. Peter's handled both adoptions. I also know you, or Father O'Malley, or whoever in God's name was in charge, never told the Greaves that their adopted daughter was

143

being adopted for the second time. I know all this for fact, and if I were really nasty, I would guess you never let Destiny see her grandmother again because you didn't want her new family to find out they had damaged goods. I don't mean to be rude, but I intend to stand here until you give me that name."

I planted myself firmly near a pint-sized drinking fountain.

At this slight threat, she collapsed.

"Her name is Frances Green, but she's not well. You should leave her in peace."

"Where can I find her?"

"I don't know."

I raised one eyebrow and tried to look menacing.

"Really, I don't know. She left the convent several years ago and broke all ties with the church. I assure you, she's not well."

By then, children in color-coordinated uniforms were running past us at break-neck speed. Over their heads, I thanked her for her time. Relieved to see me go, she slowly threaded her way back to her office.

CHAPTER

20

The next morning, I once again called the archdiocese, using a different voice and story. At the rate I was going, I was tempted to enter their number into my speed-dial phone.

A volunteer there graciously gave me Frances Green's home phone number, and I promptly put the information to use. The ex-nun herself wasn't home, but after listening to my lengthy explanation, the woman who answered her phone told me where I could find her.

Without wasting any time, I drove straight to Kennedy Golf Course. At the driving range, I easily spotted Frances Green because she was the only woman.

I must say she looked quite well to me. She was tan, fit, and dressed in dapper golf duds. She had a small, athletic body and her gray hair was cut Marine-style in a short buzz.

Her swing wasn't too shabby, either.

"Ms. Green —" I approached her.

"Fran," her deep voice boomed.

"Fran, I'm Kristin Ashe. I'm a friend of Destiny Greaves. You probably don't remember her —"

"Course I do," she interrupted.

"You handled her adoption to the Kenwood family, right?"

"Yep. My first client. Why do you want to know?"

I took a few minutes to explain how and why Destiny had hired me to look into her past.

"I hope you don't mind my coming out here. Sister Margaret

Kincaid gave me your name, and your roommate told me I could find you here."

"Surprised the old girl remembers my name. Haven't seen Sister Margaret in years."

"Good one!" I exclaimed as one of her balls soared past the two hundred yard marker.

"Why don't you join me?" She gestured expansively. "My treat. Seniors get two free buckets of balls every Wednesday and Thursday morning."

"No, really, thank you. I don't golf. Tennis is more my game."

"You any good?"

"Not bad."

"Let me guess: rapid-fire serve but it rarely goes in. Killer at the net but opponents often get you with pass-shots. Correct?"

I laughed out loud.

"You're pretty close, but you forgot to mention that I have a weak backhand."

"Didn't want to offend you." She grinned. "We should play sometime," she offered, but I couldn't tell if she was serious.

She sliced her next three drives and cursed at every one of them.

"What do you need from me, Kristin Ashe?" she asked as she reached into her bucket for three more balls.

"This is off the subject of why I came here, but why did you leave the convent?"

"I love women," she said with no trace of shame or further explanation.

I burst out laughing again, partly because I was uncomfortable with her candor, but mostly because the irony was priceless. Not well, indeed!

"No one's ever laughed that hard," she said, chuckling herself.

"Sorry," I said as I tried unsuccessfully to stop laughing.

"Don't be. Went into the convent because I loved women and left it because in the eyes of the church, I loved them too much. Guess that's funny."

"Not to some people. Sister Margaret told me you weren't well, but I'll tell you this much, I don't know what she was talking about. You look a hell of a lot better than she does."

"Happiness will do that to you." She enthusiastically hit the next three balls straight into the sky.

"But I must say, you certainly don't look like a nun, or even an ex-nun, for that matter."

"Girl, in my heyday I did. Had a hairdo that would have scared God." She let out a deep laugh.

I chuckled.

"I was thinking I'd have to meet you in a nursing home and hold your hand. And now, here I am sitting at a golfing range, watching you hit the ball farther than I can see."

"If I were any younger, I'd let you hold my hand anyway. Wouldn't that shock the good Sister Margaret?"

We laughed and laughed until the golf pro came by and asked us if we could quiet it down a bit.

In silence, except for an escaped giggle here and there, Fran Green hit the rest of the balls in her bucket, and we adjourned to the clubhouse for drinks.

"What was it like being a nun?" I asked as I took my Dr. Pepper and twisted it in my hands.

"Quite challenging really. Contrary to popular belief, we're not all teachers, and not any of us are waifs. Strongest women I met were nuns."

"What kind of work did you do for St. Peter's?"

"Handled what would now be called 'Social Services.' Worked on adoptions. Set up a soup kitchen for the homeless — first of its kind in Denver. Visited the elderly in their homes and in rest homes. Developed a prayer program for prisoners. Name it, and I probably did it," she told me as she sipped her soda.

"Destiny was your first adoption?"

"Yep. Would have handled her second adoption, too, and done a heck of a lot better job of it, except I was out of state when her parents died. In Minnesota, nursing my mother. There for almost a year before the cancer beat her."

Reflexively, I said, "I'm sorry."

She dismissed my condolences with a wave of her hand. "Don't be. Wasn't a great way to go, but it was her time."

"Did you choose the Kenwoods for Destiny?"

"In a sense, yes. But mostly, they chose each other. I knew Destiny would need more love than most babies, and when I met Peter and Barbara, I knew they could give it to her."

I was confused.

"Why did Destiny need more love — was she ill?"

"Don't you know — Destiny was a child of rape."

My eyes must have bugged out of my head. I was so shocked, I choked on my Dr. Pepper. To her credit, she immediately jumped up and came around the table to assist me.

147

"Sorry. No delicate way to put it," she said as she thumped on my back. "But I shouldn't have been so blunt."

"No kidding," I agreed as I struggled to breathe. "Her natural mother was raped?" I asked after I'd swallowed hard a few times.

She nodded.

"Tell me about it," I requested when I was done hacking, coughing and clearing my throat.

"Not much to tell. Young woman was from a prominent family in the parish. Going to school at the University of Denver when it happened. Raped by a boy who asked her out. Ending her senior year at the time, I believe."

"How tragic!"

"After the rape, she moved back with her parents. Weeks later, found out she was pregnant. They put her in isolation. Told everyone she was travelling in Europe for a year. Actually, she never left their house. One tragedy after another, that poor girl suffered. I counselled her extensively after the rape. She wanted to keep the baby, but the parents insisted she give it up for adoption."

"Abortion wasn't an option?"

"Afraid not in those days."

"So she gave her up?"

"Not easily. Gave us quite a scare there for a few days. She had an extremely difficult pregnancy and an even harder labor. After the baby was born, she wouldn't sign the papers to give her up. Cried for days about her little girl. Funny thing is, no one ever told her it was a girl. Still, she knew."

"Did you advise her to give Destiny up?"

"I did," she admitted without pride. "To this day, not sure if it was the right thing. Never forget the vacant look in her eyes the day she signed the papers. Later that afternoon, one of the nurses took me aside and told me the girl would never be able to have another child. Her insides were torn apart by the difficult birth. I'll tell you, that about ripped me in two."

"What an impossible choice the girl had!"

"It was! I encouraged her to give up the baby, because I was afraid if she kept the child, she'd never stop remembering the rape. Believe me, it was nothing you'd want to remember. It was a violent ordeal."

"Did you see the mother again, after she left the hospital?"

"No. Destiny became my first priority. Concentrated on getting her settled into her new home. Easier for me, too, I think,

148

to separate from the mother. Did hear, however, that she got married a year or two later, so maybe she found some measure of happiness. I like to think she did."

"Do you remember her name?"

"Couldn't forget it if I tried — Beth Ann Wolcott."

"Do you have any idea how I can find her?"

"Not right off the top of my head, but I'll bet I could track her down if I tried. Still got some connections in the old convent."

"Would you do that, please?"

She paused before answering. "On one condition... when I locate her, I'll have to get her permission before I'll allow you or Destiny to contact her. That's the least I can do for her. Is that fair enough?"

"More than. I'm not even sure Destiny will want to see her, but I'd like to meet her if she's willing."

She drank the last, long swig from her glass before she answered me.

"Fine. See what I can do. Maybe between the two of us, we can do something for these women."

"I hope so," I said doubtfully.

I had no idea what Frances Green and I could do twenty-nine years later for a woman who was raped and a daughter who was born out of that rape.

But I was willing to try.

CHAPTER

21

The next morning, the effects of the past finally caught up to me. I was too depressed to go to work. I called Ann and told her I wouldn't be coming into the office. If she was concerned, she didn't show it. Maybe she thought this was part of my resolve to take time off.

The new information I had about Destiny burdened me. I wanted to call her up, if for no other reason, than to get the tragic news off my chest, but I knew instinctively that it wasn't time to tell her. She'd hired me to serve as a buffer, almost like a surge protector, and I had to be just that — even if the information was frying my brain.

I wanted to meet Beth Ann Wolcott before I told Destiny about the way her life began. One sperm and one egg, violently pressed together. Frankly, it was more than I could bear to think about. I had no idea how Destiny would hold up under the news. I was hoping to present it to her at a time when I could give her some good news as well: that her mother was alive and well and wanted to meet her.

To avoid thinking about the rape, I planned my day by the *TV Guide*. I had just figured out that if I used my remote prudently, I could catch three episodes of "I Love Lucy," two talk shows, and one game of "Wheel of Fortune" when the phone rang.

I ran to get it, thinking it would be Ann with a question about work. It wasn't.

"Hello," I said, but there was no answer.

"Hello," I repeated, ready to hang up.

"It's me," came the reply at last, in a small voice.

"Jessica, hi! How are you?"

No answer.

"Are you there, Jessica?"

She giggled. I heard scuffling noises then the sound of her mother's voice.

"Hi, Kris. She wanted to call you, but as you can tell, she's not very good on the phone yet."

"That's okay, she's only four. How are they doing?"

"They're good — driving me crazy as usual. Every day they ask when they're going to see you again. I hope you don't mind, I got tired of hearing it, so I told them they could call you."

"Not at all. I've been busy lately or I would have called them," I said lamely.

"Do you think you could take them to the zoo sometime? I've been meaning to go myself, but Sam's worked every weekend, and I don't want to leave Brianna with a sitter. I've tried to explain to the kids that their three-month-old sister can't do everything they do, but you know how persistent they can be."

"I do. I'd be happy to take them. How about this Saturday? Do you have plans?"

"No, that'd be great! They'll be ready when the sun comes up, but you come on over whenever's good for you."

"How about around eleven?"

"Fine. We'll see you then."

She was getting ready to hang up when I had a great idea.

"Peggy, wait, before you go, do you think it'd be all right if I bring a friend? She's been going through some tough stuff lately. I think a day with the kids would do wonders for her."

"Not your friend Michelle, I hope."

"No, not her." The last time Michelle had come along with me and the kids, she talked about herself the whole time and repeatedly told Zeb and Jessica to be quiet when they tried to get a word in edgewise. Needless to say, they didn't like her much.

"This woman's name is Destiny."

"What a pretty name. Of course, Kris, bring her along. I'm sure the kids would love to meet your friend."

• • •

The second Peggy said good-bye, I dialed Destiny's number.

"How would you like to go to the zoo Saturday?" I asked without bothering to say "hello."

"Kris?"

"Of course it's me!"

"As long as it's you, I'd love to go. I haven't been in years."

"There's one catch...."

"What? I suppose you like to ride that stinky elephant."

"Actually, I do, but that's not the catch. The catch is that we won't be going alone." I giggled mischievously.

"Michelle's not coming, is she? Tell me you're not trying to get us back together again, Kris."

"No way! Our companions are safely out of your target market of potential lovers. They're both under the age of seven."

"Your friend Peggy's kids, Zeb and Jessica," she said, excitement replacing her earlier suspicion.

"Exactly. Will you come?"

"But your time with them is so special. I don't want to get in the way."

"You won't."

"But I haven't been around kids in years, probably not since I was a kid myself. What if they hate me?"

"They'll love you, Destiny. Just be yourself, don't use too many big words, and buy them lots of junk food. Guaranteed, they'll love you."

"I can do that," she said confidently.

"Good, I'll pick you up around ten-thirty."

"Great, I'll be ready... and thanks, Kris."

"For what?"

"For inviting me, for sharing this with me."

"Any time," I said smiling.

I got off the phone, threw the *TV Guide* in the trash, and rode my bike five miles to the Gates Tennis Center. I spent the rest of the morning hitting the ball against a backboard and smiling.

•••

I could hardly wait for Saturday to come, and when it did, I made the rounds and picked everybody up.

When I saw Destiny come running out of her house, for a split second, I felt guilty for not telling her about the rape. I wondered if she looked like her father... and I wondered what kind of a man he must have been to rape a woman. Were there traces of his

153

rage in her? All this raced through my mind before Destiny even opened the car door. When she did, her enthusiasm infected me, and I put the depressing thoughts out of my mind. Actually, it wasn't that hard for me to compartmentalize; I'd been doing it all my life.

At Peggy's house, it took a few minutes for Zeb and Jessica to warm up to Destiny. Neither one of them wanted to sit next to her in the car. She sat up front with me, and they kept each other company in the back.

Before we'd gotten very far, though, she'd won them over by helping them spot and count red cars. And when we got to the zoo, they both insisted on holding Destiny's hand.

That day was one of the best days of my life.

We spent hours walking and running and laughing. We imitated a seal, taunted a lion, and rode an elephant.

When it was time to go home, they all protested, Destiny the loudest.

Tired and sunburned and happy, we walked the longest leg of our journey — back to the car.

Once there, much scrambling took place before it was agreed that Zeb would ride shotgun and Jessica would sit in the back with Destiny. We hadn't gone far when I glanced in the rearview mirror and saw Jessica asleep with her head in Destiny's lap. Destiny was softly stroking the youngster's blonde hair. She caught me looking at her and returned my smile.

The good-byes took forever at Peggy's house, but eventually we got on the road again.

Destiny and I rode for miles in silence before I spoke.

"They liked you."

"How can you tell?"

"On the way back, they fought to sit next to you in the car. That's a good sign."

"They adore you, Kris."

"That's because I buy them lots of food."

"It's more than that, and you know it. They can't stop talking about you. They love your ghost stories."

"I am a pretty good storyteller," I conceded.

"But it's much more than even that. You love them with all your heart, and you respect them. They know that, maybe not consciously, but they know it. You explain things to them, too."

"In little words."

"In little words," she agreed.

We were both silent again as I slowly drove toward her house.

I didn't know what Destiny was thinking, but I couldn't stop thinking about Jessica. All afternoon, I had watched her, studying her with the intensity of a scholar. I watched her in all her four-year-old splendor, and I knew as I watched her that four-year-olds know.

For some reason, I had been thinking that if the bad things that happened to me had happened when I was so young, that they must not have mattered, that they couldn't have been so traumatic.

Yet, seeing Jessica, as she tore around from one place to the next, attacking life itself, I saw how aware she was.

Abuse would destroy her life, I realized, even if she couldn't remember it or understand it for another twenty years. She would never forget it. She might block it out, but she'd never completely forget.

Just as I hadn't.

She'd remember it all when she jumped at a lover's innocent touch. Or when she recoiled at a stranger's choice of words. Or when she felt uneasy because she was near the place where the loss occurred.

She'd remember it all, time after time, in shadows, the hardest kind of memories to grasp.

For a moment, I let myself feel how much Zeb and Jessica meant to me, and I wanted to cry. When it seemed as if the world were crumbling around me, I'd think of the kids. Of them running to hug me, reaching up but only grabbing my legs. Of their blonde hair. Of their brilliant questions, masked in simplicity. Of their perfect posture, spines unbent by trouble. Of their absolute, unwavering trust of adults.

I never violated that trust. I never lied to them. I never spoke to them from my own anger or pain. I never hit them. I never caressed them. But then, I wasn't their parent.

I remembered Jessica waving good-bye as we drove off, her tousled blonde hair blowing in the wind, and I knew she was safe. Her safety showed in who she was. I felt like crying for the safety I never had.

Destiny must have been reading my mind.

"When you're with them, Kris, do you ever think about yourself when you were their age?"

"All the time." I swallowed hard. "That's why I don't see them very often. It's too painful."

155

"I'll bet you were a cute kid."

"I was. You should see my baby pictures."

"I'd love to see them." She winked at me.

We both laughed because what I'd just said sounded so much like a cheap come-on.

"I didn't mean it that way."

"I know, and I didn't take it that way."

"Oh, sure," I said as I pulled into Destiny's driveway. We both laughed again.

"Thanks for a great day, Kris," she said and gave me a hug.

"You're very welcome," I answered, feeling her warmth.

As she was closing the car door, she said, so quietly I could barely hear her, "I haven't felt this good in a long time."

Before I could answer, she was off running up her steps. I wanted to run after her, but I didn't.

Little did I know then that the next time I was to see her would be under the strangest of circumstances. If I had known, I probably would have gone inside and held her all night long, sheltering her from what was to come.

• • •

When I got home, there was a message on my phone machine from Fran Green. I let out a little yelp, then ran to my bedroom to hunt for her phone number. When I found it, I rang her immediately.

"Fran Green here."

"Hi, Fran, it's Kristin Ashe. How's your search coming?"

"Quite well, actually! Located Beth Ann Wolcott," she said, sounding pleased with herself.

"You're kidding! That was fast! How'd you do it?"

"Called in a few markers at the convent. Denver's just one big small town, and the longer you live here, the smaller it gets."

"Is she still living in Denver?" I couldn't believe my luck. Frances Green was finishing up this case for me.

"Certainly is. Never left the city. Been married and divorced and raised a daughter herself."

"You're kidding! Tell me everything."

"Called her today. Must say, gave her the shock of her life. Right away, she knew who I was. Remembered the counseling sessions we had."

I couldn't stand the suspense!

156

"Does she want to meet Destiny?"

"You're getting ahead of my story."

"C'mon, Fran, give!"

"Yep!"

"All right!" I let out my loudest, most joyful scream.

"Hold up," she cautioned me.

"What?" I asked, all worried.

"In the interest of discretion, I didn't tell her anything about Destiny — not her name, not her job, nothing. Didn't want to shock Beth Ann, finding out her baby turned out to be the most famous lesbian in Denver. Figured the two of them could work it out on their own after they meet."

"Good thinking. I'm just glad she wants to meet her. Did she ever think of looking for Destiny herself?"

"Couldn't. Legally, no way for her to find her. That's why she was delighted I called. Kids can look for their parents, but parents can't look for their kids."

"I suppose that's to protect the child."

"Suppose. At any rate, Beth Ann's going to give her ex-husband a buzz. Wants to talk to him before she meets Destiny."

"Why?"

"Poor girl never told him about the rape or the child. Held in the secret for all these years... can't imagine it."

"I can imagine," I replied, thinking of the duration of my own secrecy. "But why tell him now?"

"Seems they're good friends. Been through some rough times lately, with their daughter I gathered. Beth Ann didn't say."

"When will she meet Destiny?"

"As soon as she talks to her ex. I'm supposed to call tonight to set up a time."

"Do you think she'd agree to meet me first — alone?"

"Might. But why go without Destiny?"

"Destiny hired me specifically to put distance between herself and the people in her past. I'm supposed to do the initial screening. After I meet Beth Ann, I'll present all the facts to Destiny and let her decide if she wants to meet her."

"Chance she might not want to?"

"Maybe."

"Hope that's not the case, Kristin. I called this woman in good faith, trying to do some good for both of them. Hate to tell her now her daughter doesn't want to meet her."

"It probably won't come to that, Fran."

"I don't like this, but I'll call her."

"Neither do I, but I have to protect Destiny."

"I'd like to protect Beth Ann myself."

"Don't worry — I'll be careful with her."

"Better be. Talk to you later."

As I look back on it now, it's almost funny how I tried so hard to keep all the emotional pieces of Destiny's life organized in a logical way. Of course it didn't work.

In the end, nothing went according to plan, starting with my intention to get a lot of sleep that night because I had a busy day ahead of me at Marketing Consultants.

Ann and I are at my parents' house, and I'm on the phone with one of my Marketing Consultants clients. I'm in my mom's bedroom upstairs. Ann's downstairs. Dad keeps coming down the hall and revealing himself to me. I keep him at bay by holding my hand over the phone and screaming at him that I'll tell Ann, that I'll call the police.

All the while, I'm trying to keep my client from knowing. Somehow, I feel responsible because I let my father start this by letting him do something that seemed inappropriate but not terrifying, then it got out of hand.

When Ann comes upstairs, I tell her what Dad did. He tries to deny it, tries to tell her that I came on to him.

Somehow, we kick this man out of the house. We file a report that doesn't press charges but does go on file. The abuse is on record.

• • •

My Monday went quickly. After Fran called to tell me I could meet Beth Ann Wolcott the next day, I soared through the rest of my work. I only took time out to call Destiny and tell her the good news, that I'd be meeting her mother the next day. She asked if I'd found out anything about her father. I lied and said no, that maybe her mother could shed some light on him.

All night, I paid for my lying as I tossed and turned, practicing different ways of breaking the news to Destiny that her father was a rapist. By dawn, I still hadn't come up with a good way to phrase such a fact.

CHAPTER

22

Tuesday, every hour seemed like a week as I waited for my afternoon visit with Destiny's mother. When at last I arrived at her house, I let out a short whistle. Beth Ann Wolcott had done quite well for herself. Her home was a mansion located in the affluent Greenwood Village enclave. I parked my car in the circular driveway, walked up to the door and, with butterflies in my stomach, gave the brass doorknocker a decisive clang.

I was nervous because Fran Green hadn't exactly paved the way for my arrival. When she'd called back to tell me a time and address, she made it quite clear that Beth Ann was upset that she'd have to meet me first. She'd been expecting to meet directly with her daughter. Frankly, I couldn't see what the big deal was. She'd waited this long. What was one more day? And wouldn't it be easier for her, too, I rationalized, if she was able to meet a friend of Destiny's before she actually met Destiny. Evidently not, according to Fran.

I barely had time to process these thoughts because the door opened so quickly I could only guess Beth Ann had been watching me from the window in the entry.

"Hi, I'm Kristin Ashe. I think Fran Green told you about me," I began as a means of introduction.

Her first words were nothing like I expected.

"I can't talk to you right now," came the frightened voice from behind the mostly closed door. She'd opened it a crack so she could see me, but I couldn't see much of her.

"But didn't Fran call you," I protested, my heart sinking.

"I want to talk to you," she whispered urgently, "but this really isn't a good time right now. I hate to inconvenience you, but do you think you could come back in a few hours?"

"I've driven a long way to get here," I lied. I was afraid if I went away, she'd never allow me back.

"I'm sorry, I thought this would be a good time, but it's not. My daughter stopped by a few minutes ago. It was quite unexpected. We haven't even spoken to one another in several weeks. She's up in her room now, going through some of her old things, but she could come down any minute. I hope you can understand."

The light bulb finally went off in my head.

"And you haven't told her anything about this other child of yours, right?"

"Correct. I was going to, but I wanted to be sure you'd come first before I upset anyone."

"I understand perfectly," I said graciously and prepared to quickly depart. "If she sees me leaving, tell her I'm a Jehovah's Witness who tried to lead you to the Lord."

"I will." She gave me a faint smile.

My back was turned, and I was stepping off the porch when I heard the sound of her daughter's voice.

"Hey, Mom, look what I found...."

The innocent voice of the daughter she never told. The voice that froze all time and thoughts for me.

The voice that was Destiny's.

At first I thought it was a joke, that somehow Destiny had located her birth mother on her own and wanted to play a practical joke on me.

But then I saw all color drain from her mother's face, and I knew it wasn't a joke.

The scene that followed will be etched in my mind until the day I die.

I must have spun around. Beth Ann Wolcott turned white and tried to close the door. Destiny realized someone was at the door and came to see who it was. When she saw me, her face registered surprise, then happiness, then terror.

She knew what I'd set out to do that afternoon. In her eyes, I could see her realize why I was there.

Beth Ann Wolcott, the woman who had adopted her and cared for her for twenty-five years, was also the woman who had abandoned her twenty-nine years ago.

Destiny didn't have three mothers. She only had two.

Destiny looked ill. Her mother looked ill. I couldn't see myself, but I'm sure I looked ill, too — I felt sick enough. I'm surprised I didn't faint. I think it's a testament to my coping ability that I managed to stay on my feet.

After what seemed like hours, but probably was only seconds, we all started speaking at once.

"Kris, this can't be!" Destiny said in a voice that absolutely broke my heart.

"I'm so sorry, Destiny."

"Destiny, I'd like you to meet Kristin Ashe, a Jehovah's Witness who stopped by —" her mother started to say.

And then it dawned on her that Destiny and I already knew each other. "But how do you two know each other? Have you met?"

"God, no, Kris, God no!"

"Destiny, I'm sorry!"

After much jostling, I finally managed to get in the door, past her protective mother. I took Destiny in my arms and held her tight. Without sound, she was sobbing. I could feel every emotion in her body.

Over her shoulder, I said to Beth Ann Wolcott, aka Liz Greaves, that Destiny was the one who had hired me.

At that, Destiny's mother fainted. She managed to get herself into the living room and onto a sofa before she actually passed out, which was fortunate, because I was in no position to offer her assistance. I was too busy propping up Destiny.

As soon as it seemed safe to walk, I helped Destiny into the living room and put her on the sofa next to her mother, then I went in search of the kitchen. When I found it, I located two glasses, filled them with water, and brought them into the living room. I gave Destiny hers and then tried to revive her mother.

"Destiny is my real daughter?" were the first words she spoke when she woke up, and they were spoken more from a place of horror than joy.

"She is. The Kenwoods were the couple who adopted her from you, and as you know, they died in a car crash four years later."

"I never knew their name," she gasped.

"I'm sorry for what you've gone through," I said and I was.

I didn't like Liz Greaves. From the minute Destiny described her, I disliked her for her overbearing control and her inability to love Destiny. But Beth Ann Wolcott, that was a different story. She had made the choice to give up her child, but what a choice! When I was young, I'd thought there were good choices and bad choices. As I grew older, I came to realize that many of life's choices were between a bad option and one that was worse. That was the sort of choice Beth Ann had faced.

No wonder she was unable to love Destiny.

"I don't know what to call you," I said, which may have been a stupid thing to say under the circumstances, but it was all that came to mind. Liz? Mrs. Greaves? Beth Ann? Ms. Wolcott? What would it be?

"Liz. My formal name is Elizabeth Ann. Beth Ann's a nickname my family used. Beth Ann died the night it happened."

She never said what "it" was, but I knew she was referring to the rape. Destiny probably thought she was referring to the night she had to give up her daughter.

Destiny was lying in a fetal position on the couch, her body turned away from her mother, not saying a word.

"I'm so sorry, Destiny," her mother said and reached to touch her daughter's legs, but Destiny pulled away from her.

Wiping at the tears streaming down her face, Liz Greaves turned to me but clearly directed her words to Destiny.

"I thought this would be the happiest day of my life. I never thought I'd see my daughter again. It was especially painful for me when you started looking for your real mother, Destiny. I felt worse than ever, very sorry for myself. I was jealous of you. I've always wanted to look for my daughter, from the day I gave her, gave you, away, but I knew I never could. When Sister Frances called, I thought it was a miracle... and now this!"

Neither mother nor daughter seemed happy to have found each other, and I can't say I was thrilled that I was the one who had made all this possible.

Without a word to me or her mother, Destiny got up and left the room. I started to follow her, but her words and the coldness in her tone stopped me.

"Don't come, Kris. I want to be alone."

I sat down, or more like fell down, on the part of the couch she'd just vacated, not knowing what to do. Some people say they want to be alone when in fact they really need and want someone to be with them. Other people say they want to be alone and that's exactly what they mean. I wasn't sure which kind of person Destiny was, so I sought her mom's opinion.

"Should I follow her?"

"She's too stubborn. She always has been," her mother said with a trace of disdain.

"I don't think she should be alone right now. Maybe I should go after her."

"Give her a few minutes headstart, that's what her father and I used to do, then follow her. I know exactly where she's going," she sniffled.

"Where?"

"There's a park a few blocks from here. When she was little and she ran away from home, which was quite often, we always found her at the park."

"Could you give me directions."

Liz Greaves gave me directions but then wouldn't let me leave.

"I wanted to keep her you know, but my family wouldn't permit it."

"Yes, Fran Green told me that," I said with perhaps not enough sympathy.

"It wasn't my family, though, not really."

"I know. Fran told me everything," I said, hoping to cut her off because I didn't think I could bear to listen to what was about to follow.

"She couldn't have told you everything," she said in a sing-song voice. "She didn't know everything. I didn't tell her what it felt like to be violated, to have him constantly thrusting himself at me, over and over again, until I suffocated inside. She couldn't have told you that because I never told anyone."

"I'm sorry, Liz."

"Beth Ann Wolcott *did* die that night. And even though I couldn't bear to look at a child that was from his ugly seed, I never stopped missing my baby. She was mine, too. No one seemed to understand that. I gave away an evil man when I gave her away, but I gave away some of me, too."

"I'm sorry for you and for Destiny. I truly am." I stood up to leave. Awkwardly, I said, "I think I should be going now. I'd like to be with Destiny."

"Don't go yet."

"I think I should."

"But I'd like to talk to you. I have so many questions," she begged.

"When you can, Liz, ask Destiny the questions. She can answer them better than I can."

I started walking toward the door and made the mistake of walking by Liz Greaves. In desperation, she grabbed my arm.

"One question, please answer one question for me. I did agree to meet with you today. You owe me that much," she pleaded.

"Okay," I agreed, more so she'd let go of my arm than because I really felt like I owed her something.

"Why did she do it?"

"Do what?"

"Why did Destiny want to find her real mother? Why wasn't I enough for her?" was her haunting question.

"Probably for the same reason you wanted to find your real daughter," I said quietly, and then I pulled my arm away from her and walked out of there as fast as my legs could carry me. Her words chased me down the hall.

"But I tried to be a good mother. That's all I ever wanted to be, a good mother. I was involved in every aspect of Destiny's life. I gave her all the things I couldn't give my baby...."

And then you resented her for having them, I thought wryly as I closed the front door.

When I got outside, I couldn't help but look back at the house and think of all the pain it had held inside it for so many years. Pain that no one ever talked about. Destiny privately grieving, even though she was just a little kid. Liz Greaves privately grieving.

Suddenly, I couldn't bear the thought of all the sadness that lay beyond those walls. Behind the painted shutters. Behind the symmetrically placed bricks. Behind the picture windows. Behind all the things that made the place look inviting, there was so much pain.

CHAPTER

23

I was in no mood to walk, so I drove the short distance to the park. I found Destiny exactly where her mother had said she would be. She was alone on the playground, sitting in one of the swings, not moving. I parked my car and walked toward her. When I was about halfway there, she saw me but didn't say anything. I raised my hand slightly and gave a little wave. She nodded grimly.

I delicately picked my way through the mud, trying to keep as much of it as possible off my bare ankles and my blue jeans.

"Hi," I tentatively said when I got near her. "Your mom told me I might find you here. Is it okay if I stay?"

She didn't say anything but nodded her head ever so slightly. I sat in the swing next to her. Every few minutes I looked over at her, but she never looked at me. She stared straight ahead as if I wasn't there until at last she spoke, and when she did, her words came out in a torrent.

"I can't believe she's my mother! Why didn't she ever tell me she had a daughter? Does my father know?"

I shook my head and by my silence, forced her to look at me.

"Why not? Why didn't she tell him? My God, I hope he's not my real father. He isn't, is he, Kris? Tell me he didn't give me away, too!"

I shook my head again.

I seemed incapable of finding the words I needed to tell her the horrible truth.

"Then who is my father? Does my mother even know who fucked her?"

I winced at the brutality in her words and took a deep breath.

"Your mother was raped, and then she became pregnant," I said quietly, blinking rapidly.

"No!" she screamed, a sound more primal than any I'd ever heard. "No! No! No!"

Each scream felt like someone was kicking me in the stomach.

"No! No! No!" Her emotion seemed to create a fence around the swing set. Just she and I and all the pain were inside the fence. I wanted desperately to be on the other side, but I couldn't move. My eyes were riveted on Destiny as she stood and violently shook her head back and forth. She kept grabbing her hair and letting go of it in slow, exaggerated motions.

I got up and moved toward her to try to calm her, to offer some kind of physical comfort, but she stepped back, as if in a trance.

I didn't know what else to do, what else to offer her, so I gave her what I give best: words.

Between screams, I talked to her. Standing right there in the middle of this children's playground, I rambled on and on. About everything. About nothing I can remember now.

Gradually, and I mean gradually, because it seemed to happen at an agonizingly slow pace, her screams became softer and her body movements grew less violent.

Eventually, she staggered back to the grassy, snow-covered area and crumpled to the ground. Slowly, cautiously, talking all the while, I approached her. This time, she let me near.

I helped her get up from the ground and steered her to a park bench a few feet from where she'd fallen. I gently sat her down, and then I sank down next to her.

I stopped talking after she let out her last scream and in the silence, I could no longer ignore the pain that was in and around me. We sat there, not talking, our legs barely touching, until without sound, I lowered my head and started to cry.

I cried for Destiny Greaves, and I cried for myself. For in us, I saw the struggle, and I realized it would be there for a lifetime.

"I can't take much more of this, Kris. I truly cannot."

I raised my head and laughed nervously at her extreme understatement.

"I think we're about done, Destiny. Unless you want me to look into your grandparents' lives or something," I mustered up enough energy to make a feeble joke as I used my shirt collar to

166

wipe away my tears.

"Just my luck — they're probably murderers," she said angrily and then added, "How long have you known about the rape, Kris?"

"Since the day I met Fran Green."

"Why didn't you tell me before now? Did you ever intend to tell me or were you, too, going to be the keeper of the little secret?"

"Of course I was going to tell you," I responded to her anger with some of my own. "You hired me because you wanted distance. I gave you that distance by holding on to your 'little secret,' as you call it, until I thought you were ready for it."

"When, just when, did you think I'd be ready to hear that I am what's left of a rape that happened thirty years ago?"

She had me there.

"I was going to tell you after I met your mother, so I could give you some good news along with the bad news," I said, and as I said it, the plan sounded lame even to me.

"You are some kind of caretaker, Kristin Ashe," she said bitterly, and I knew she meant it as an insult.

"I am," I agreed without shame. "That's why you hired me, Destiny Greaves. You needed some caretaking."

At that, she burst into wild laughter.

"What's so funny?" I asked, concerned by the edge of hysteria that I heard in her laugh.

"Nothing's funny. Absolutely nothing," she muttered as she stood up abruptly.

"Where are you going?" I asked in a voice that must have revealed alarm.

"Calm down, Kris. You're like a mother hen. I'm just going to go swing for a while. Right over there." She pointed to the swings. "You can watch me the whole time. You can even join me if you'd like."

"Thanks, I think I'll watch."

"Suit yourself," she said as she sprinted off.

Once she got to the swing, she didn't waste any time. She started swinging fast and furiously. In her frenzy, she was almost graceful. Seeing her fly high up into the sky, I remembered all the times I'd jumped from swings when I was a kid, always seeing if I could jump just a little farther. As I watched Destiny swing, I hoped she wouldn't jump. Surely she would have hurt herself from that height.

"Do you think I look like her?" she shouted at me.

I didn't know what to answer. I tried to think of the reply that would cause her the least amount of pain, but I couldn't imagine what that would be. In the end, I opted for the truth.

"A little."

That obviously didn't please her. She continued to frantically pump her legs, her long blonde hair streaming behind her.

She didn't say anything more after that.

I moved to the merry-go-round and tried to think of what I could say to this woman who had lost and found so many mothers in such a short period of time. Not surprisingly, nothing came to me, so I just sat there for the longest time, feeling very alone.

The playground reminded me of my first girlfriend. We met in the third grade. Her name was Sharon Seabaugh, but I called her Sharon Snowball. By the time we were in sixth grade, she'd had three different names. She was Sharon Seabaugh, Sharon Smith and Sharon Cavanaugh, and by her third name, she was getting into all kinds of trouble. Today, her uncontrollable behavior would be given a fancy name, and she'd be put in a special learning program for disturbed children. Back then, we just thought she had a screwed-up mother who got married too often.

I wondered how Sharon had turned out.

And what her name was.

I was hunched over, arms folded, elbows resting on my thighs, when I felt Destiny's hand on my shoulder.

"Hey, aren't your feet cold?" she asked.

I looked up. "A little," I said and smiled. Much to my relief, she smiled back.

"Don't they freeze in the winter when you don't wear socks?"

"You get used to it after awhile," I said between sniffles. "Like the first day you go barefoot, your feet are tender, but by the end of the summer, they're rock hard. Same thing with temperature. I get so I don't notice."

"Why don't you wear socks?"

"I don't know. I never have. Probably related to my dysfunctional childhood somehow. I haven't made the connection yet, but I'm sure it's my parents' fault." I smiled.

"Isn't it always? All parents fail their children, Kris. They should have the nurse tell you that the second you're born."

"Good idea, it's true isn't it? And I suppose children fail their parents. By the way, don't your legs hurt from swinging?"

"Not as much as the rest of me." She hopped on the merry-go-round and sat with her legs straddling the silver bar and her chin resting on the cold steel. She started to move the merry-go-round, but I asked her to stop.

The motion surely would have made me sick.

I was going to ask her if she thought the pain would ever go away, but she spoke first, and I never did get the answer I desperately needed.

"It's funny, Kris, when I was growing up, every time someone remarked how much I looked like her, it made me sick because I knew I couldn't possibly look like her — she wasn't my real mother. My mother, the one I looked like, was dead. I wanted to tell everyone who said that to me. But I never did. Every time they'd comment on the resemblance, I'd wish I was her real daughter so she wouldn't look so sad. She tried to hide the hurt look in her eyes, but I always saw it. And you know what —those looks couldn't possibly compare to the look I saw in her eyes today when she found out I *was* her daughter. That's a hell of a note, isn't it?"

"I think she was just shocked, not disappointed," I lied.

"Did I look hurt, too?"

"A little."

"Of course, I did. How could I not? For years, I wanted her, Liz Greaves, to be my real mother. And obviously, she wanted me to be her real daughter. And now that we've found each other, we feel horrible. Isn't that just the most fucked up thing you've ever heard of?

"This is the end of the line — no more mothers to track down. She's the only one I'll ever have, and blood ties or not, she's not enough. Just because I discovered today that I came from her flesh, she didn't magically become enough mother. I still desperately miss this 'fantasy mother' that I think would have given me all the things she couldn't."

She paused.

"Do you think Barbara Kenwood would have been a better mother if she'd lived?"

Now how on earth could I answer that question?

"I don't know, Destiny. She loved you a lot, but that's not always enough."

"It's a hell of a good start!"

"True."

She paused again, her brow furrowed in thought.

"This searching, Kris, is it really worth it? Do you think we've accomplished anything by it?"

"Of course we have! You have hope now, hope that what happened to you as a child can finally stop consuming you as an adult. Because as much as you tried to suppress the memories, they're the only thing that can help you figure out why you act crazy sometimes. You've finally stopped running from the pain. That's what you've accomplished. And I've accomplished it, too. The world is changing — we're changing it!"

"Maybe it was better when we were running."

"God, no! How can you say that? You're the one who got me to stop running, the only one I trusted enough to slow down for. And I stopped running long enough to tell you I'd been abused, something I'd never been able to admit before. The day I told you, Destiny, is the day I finally started the long, slow process of healing.

"It probably doesn't seem like it, but you found out some things today that might give you more peace than you've ever had. Don't you see, the way your mother treated you was a reflection of her own failings, not yours. Same with my father. We weren't bad. They simply weren't good enough.

"Now you know why it was hard for your mother to accept you. She couldn't love you like she should have because she wanted you to be her real daughter. And you also know why your birth mother deserted you. Because she was raped and every time she looked at you, she would have been reminded of the assault. I agree it's extremely weird that both these mothers happen to be the same woman, but at least you have some resolution. And maybe now, you and your mom can work on improving your relationship."

"Maybe," she said begrudgingly. "I still can't believe she didn't tell my dad, though!"

"Was he the kind of man who could understand what it felt like to be raped, and then to have to bear the child of your rapist?" I asked, able to guess the answer for myself.

"Probably not," she said, and for the first time, I heard a hint of compassion for her mother.

I freed myself from the merry-go-round and stood up.

"We should probably be getting back to your mom's. Do you think you're ready?"

"I suppose. I guess I have to face her sometime."

We started back toward the car. As we walked, I lightly draped my arm around her shoulders. She let it stay there.

"I've got a long way to go, don't I?"

"Probably, but you've come a long way, too."

She was silent for a moment, as if pondering the accuracy of what I'd said.

"I guess I have, haven't I? I forget that sometimes."

"You're a fighter. You always have been. You had the courage to survive. So did I. Now we have to find the courage to thrive."

"That's the harder part," she said.

We walked along in silence.

And then, out of the blue, in a voice full of self-confidence that didn't seem to belong to me, I said, "Let's do it, Destiny, let's make love." I tried to keep my tone lighthearted, but even I could hear how serious my request sounded.

She stopped dead in her tracks, looked straight at me, and shook her head. "You know I'm not ready for that, Kris."

"But I feel like *I* am!" I practically shouted, filling the park with the sounds of joy and wonderment.

"Damn, you want to and I don't. That must mean we're both healing, but when are we ever going to be ready to do it at the same time?"

I shrugged my shoulders, and we both laughed.

"I'm glad you're in my life, Kris," she said as she hugged me tightly.

"Me, too, Destiny."

I closed my eyes and held on for a long time.

Jennifer L. Jordan

Jennifer L. Jordan was born, raised and still resides in Denver, Colorado. She's an entrepreneur who started her first business when she was eighteen.

For the past eight years, she's made her living as a self-employed, self-taught technical writer and graphic designer. She currently owns and operates two businesses.

In her spare time, she collects watches, goes to hundreds of movies a year, rides her mountain bike 50 miles a week, and trys to keep her lover from adopting any more stray animals.

This is her first novel.

Our Power Press

Our Power Press is dedicated to changing the world, one book at a time. We'll do this by publishing extraordinary lesbian novels and mysteries.

Periodically, we'll be sending out newsletters and announcements. If you'd like to be on our mailing list, please send your name and address to:

Our Power Press
P.O. Box 6680
Denver, Colorado 80206